MABINOGION LEGENDS:

KILHWCH AND OLWEN
PEREDUR THE SON OF EVRAWC
LLUDD AND LLEVELYS
TALIESIN.

Also published by Llanerch:

MABINOGION: THE FOUR BRANCHES
translated by Charlotte Guest
with drawings by Jo Nathan.

MABINOGION TALES
translated by Charlotte Guest
with illustrations by Jo Nathan.

PEREDUR: AN ARTHURIAN ROMANCE
FROM THE MABINOGION
translated by Meirion Pennar
with drawings by James Negus.

SYMBOLISM OF THE CELTIC CROSS
by Derek Bryce
with drawings by J. Romilly Allen and others.

THE CHRONICLE OF ADAM OF USK
translated by E. M. Thompson.

From booksellers. For a complete list,
write to LLANERCH PUBLISHERS,
Felinfach, Lampeter, Dyfed, SA48 8PJ.

MABINOGION LEGENDS:
KILHWCH AND OLWEN
PEREDUR THE SON OF EVRAWC
LLUDD AND LLEVELYS
TALIESIN.

TRANSLATED FROM THE RED BOOK OF HERGEST
BY LADY CHARLOTTE GUEST.
EDITED BY OWEN EDWARDS,
WITH DRAWINGS BY JO CONTI.

ISBN 0947992 97 9
Facsimile reprint with new illustrations
by LLANERCH PUBLISHERS, Felinfach, 1992.

4   CONTENTS:

Lady Charlotte Guest has given the *Mabinogion* to English readers in the form which, probably, will always delight them. Her transcript of the *Red Book of Hergest* was not perfect, she found the meaning of many a Welsh phrase obscure, but her rendering is generally very accurate; and the Celtic tales retain in their new dress much of the charm, which so often evades a translator, of a perfect style formed by generations of narrating.

In this edition of Lady Guest's translation I have put, in the form of footnotes, what appears to me to be a more correct or literal rendering of some of the passages of the Welsh. This course makes it unnecessary to tamper with the charming translation that has become a classic of the English Language.

OWEN EDWARDS.

Lincoln College, Oxford. 1st. March 1902.

KILHWCH AND OLWEN

OR THE

TWRCH TRWYTH

KILYDD, the son of Prince Kelyddon desired a wife as a helpmate, and the wife that he chose was Goleuddydd, the daughter of Prince Anlawdd. And after their union the people put up prayers that they might have an heir. And they had a son through the prayers of the people. From the time of her pregnancy Goleuddydd became wild, and wandered about, without habitation; but when her delivery was at hand, her reason came back to her. Then she went to a mountain where there was a swineherd, keeping a herd of swine. And through fear of the swine the queen was delivered. And the swineherd took the boy, and brought him to the palace ; and he was christened, and they called him Kilhwch, because he had been found in a swine's burrow. Nevertheless the boy was of gentle lineage, and cousin unto Arthur ; and they put him out to nurse.

After this the boy's mother, Goleuddydd, the daughter of Prince Anlawdd, fell sick. Then she called her husband unto her, and said to him, "Of this sickness I shall die, and thou wilt take another wife. Now wives are the gift of the Lord, but it would be wrong for thee to harm thy son. Therefore I charge thee that thou take not a wife until thou see a briar with two blossoms upon my grave." And this he promised her. Then she besought him to dress her grave every year, that nothing might grow thereon.[1] So the queen died. Now the king sent an attendant every morning to see if anything were growing upon the grave. And at the end of the seventh year the master neglected that which he had promised to the queen.

One day the king went to hunt, and he rode to the place of burial, to see the grave, and to know if it were time that he should take a wife ; and the king saw the briar. And when he saw it, the king took counsel where he should find a wife. Said one of his counsellors, "I know a wife that will suit thee well, and she is the wife of King Doged." And they resolved to go to seek her ; and they slew the king,

[1] And what she did was to call her tutor to her, and she commanded him to dress her grave every year in such a way that nothing would grow on it.

and brought away his wife and one daughter that she had along with her. And they conquered the king's lands.

On a certain day as the lady walked abroad, she came to the house of an old crone that dwelt in the town, and that had no tooth in her head. And the queen said to her, "Old woman, tell me that which I shall ask thee, for the love of Heaven. Where are the children of the man who has carried me away by violence?" Said the crone, "He has not children." Said the queen, "Woe is me, that I should have come to one who is childless!" Then said the hag, "Thou needest not lament on account of that, for there is a prediction that he shall have an heir by thee, and by none other. Moreover, be not sorrowful, for he has one son."

The lady returned home with joy, and she asked her consort, "Wherefore hast thou concealed thy children from me?" The king said, "I will do so no longer." And he sent messengers for his son, and he was brought to the Court. His stepmother said unto him, "It were well for thee to have a wife, and I have a daughter who is sought of every man of renown in the world." "I am not yet of an age to wed," answered the youth. Then said she unto him, "I declare to thee, that it is thy destiny not to be suited with a wife until thou obtain Olwen, the daughter of Yspaddaden Penkawr." And the youth blushed, and the love of the maiden diffused itself through all his frame, although he had never seen her. And his father enquired of him, "What has come over thee, my son, and what aileth thee?" "My stepmother has declared to me, that I shall never have a wife until I obtain Olwen, the daughter of Yspaddaden Penkawr." "That will be easy for thee," answered

E

his father. "Arthur is thy cousin. Go, therefore,
unto Arthur, to cut thy hair, and ask this of him as a
boon."

And the youth pricked forth upon a steed with head
dappled grey, of four winters old, firm of limb, with
shell-formed hoofs, having a bridle of linked gold on
his head, and upon him a saddle of costly gold. And
in the youth's hand were two spears of silver, sharp,
well-tempered, headed with steel, three ells in length,
of an edge to wound the wind, and cause blood to
flow, and swifter than the fall[1] of the dew-drop from
the blade of reed grass upon the earth, when the dew

of June is at the heaviest. A gold-hilted sword was
upon his thigh, the blade of which was of gold,
bearing a cross of inlaid gold of the hue of the light-
ning of heaven : his war-horn was of ivory. Before
him were two brindled white-breasted greyhounds,
having strong collars of rubies about their necks,
reaching from the shoulder to the ear. And the one

[1] And there were two silver spears, sharpened, in his hand.
A prince's glaive was in his hand, a cubit from hilt to edge, that
would draw blood from the wind ; swifter was it than

that was on the left side bounded across to the right
side, and the one on the right to the left, and like two
sea swallows sported around him.   And his courser
cast up four sods with his four hoofs, like four
swallows in the air, about his head, now above, now
below.   About him was a four-cornered cloth of
purple, and an apple of gold was at each corner; and
every one of the apples was of the value of an hundred
kine.   And there was precious gold of the value of
three hundred kine upon his shoes, and upon his
stirrups, from his knee to the tip of his toe.   And the
blade of grass bent not beneath him, so light was his
courser's tread as he journeyed towards the gate of
Arthur's palace.

Spoke the youth, " Is there a porter ? "   " There
is ; and if thou holdest not thy peace, small will be
thy welcome.[1]   I am Arthur's porter every first day of
January.   And during every other part of the year
but this the office is filled by Huandaw, and Gogigwc,
and Llaeskenym, and Pennpingyon, who goes upon
his head to save his feet, neither towards the sky nor
towards the earth, but like a rolling stone upon the
floor of the Court."   " Open the portal."   " I will
not open it."   " Wherefore not ? "   " The knife is in
the meat, and the drink is in the horn, and there is
revelry in Arthur's hall, and none may enter therein
but the son of a king of a privileged country, or a
craftsman bringing his craft.   But there will be re-
freshment for thy dogs, and for thy horses ; and for
thee there will be collops cooked and peppered, and
luscious wine and mirthful songs, and food for fifty
men shall be brought unto thee in the guest chamber,
where the stranger and the sons of other countries eat,

[1] Yes.   And as for thee, thy head is not under thy control ;
curt is thy greeting.

who come not unto the precincts of the Palace of
Arthur.   Thou wilt fare no worse there than thou
wouldest with Arthur in the Court.   A lady shall
smooth thy couch, and shall lull thee with songs; and
early to-morrow morning, when the gate is open for
the multitude that came hither to-day, for thee shall
it be opened first, and thou mayest sit in the place
that thou shalt choose in Arthur's Hall, from the
upper end to the lower."   Said the youth, "That will
I not do.   If thou openest the gate, it is well.   If
thou dost not open it, I will bring disgrace upon thy
Lord, and evil report upon thee.   And I will set up
three shouts at this very gate, than which none were
ever more deadly, from the top of Pengwaed in
Cornwall to the bottom of Dinsol, in the North, and
to Esgair Oervel, in Ireland.   And all the women in
this Palace that are pregnant shall lose their offspring;
and such as are not pregnant, their hearts shall be
turned by illness, so that they shall never bear
children from this day forward."   "What clamour
soever thou mayest make," said Glewlwyd Gavaelvawr,
"against the laws of Arthur's Palace, shalt thou not
enter therein, until I first go and speak with Arthur."

Then Glewlwyd went into the Hall.   And Arthur
said to him, "Hast thou news from the gate?"—
"Half of my life is past, and half of thine.   I was
heretofore in Kaer Se and Asse, in Sach and Salach,
in Lotor and Fotor; and I have been heretofore in
India the Great and India the Lesser; and I was in
the battle of Dau Ynyr, when the twelve hostages
were brought from Llychlyn.   And I have also been
in Europe, and in Africa, and in the Islands of
Corsica, and in Caer Brythwch, and Brythach, and
Verthach; and I was present when formerly thou
didst slay the family of Clis the son of Merin, and

when thou didst slay Mil Du, the son of Ducum, and
when thou didst conquer Greece in the East.   And I
have been in Caer Oeth and Annoeth, and in Caer
Nevenhyr ; nine supreme sovereigns, handsome men,
saw we there, but never did I behold a man of equal
dignity with him who is now at the door of the
portal."   Then said Arthur, "If walking thou didst
enter in here, return thou running.   And every one
that beholds the light, and every one that opens and
shuts the eye, let him show him respect, and serve
him, some with gold-mounted drinking horns, others
with collops cooked and peppered, until food and
drink can be prepared for him.   It is unbecoming to
keep such a man as thou sayest he is in the wind and
the rain."   Said Kai, "By the hand of my friend, if
thou wouldest follow my counsel, thou wouldest not
break through the laws of the Court because of him."
"Not so, blessed Kai, it is an honour to us to be re-
sorted to, and the greater our courtesy, the greater
will be our renown, and our fame, and our glory."

   And Glewlwyd came to the gate, and opened the
gate before him ; and although all dismounted upon
the horse-block at the gate, yet did he not dismount,
but he rode in upon his charger.   Then said Kilhwch,
"Greeting be unto thee, Sovereign Ruler of this
Island ; and be this greeting no less unto the lowest
than unto the highest, and be it equally unto thy
guests, and thy warriors, and thy chieftains—let all
partake of it as completely as thyself.   And complete
be thy favour, and thy fame, and thy glory, throughout
all this Island."   "Greeting unto thee also," said
Arthur, "sit thou between two of my warriors, and
thou shalt have minstrels before thee, and thou shalt
enjoy the privileges of a king born to a throne, as long
as thou remainest here.   And when I dispense my

presents to the visitors and strangers in this Court, they shall be in thy hand at my commencing." Said the youth, "I came not here to consume meat and drink; but if I obtain the boon that I seek, I will requite it thee, and extol thee; and if I have it not, I will bear forth thy dispraise to the four quarters of the world, as far as thy renown has extended." Then said Arthur, " Since thou wilt not remain here, chieftain, thou shalt receive the boon whatsoever thy tongue may name, as far as the wind dries and the rain moistens, and the sun revolves, and the sea encircles, and the earth extends; save only my ship; and my mantle; and Caledvwlch, my sword, and Rhongomyant, my lance; and Wynebgwrthucher, my shield; and Carnwenhau,[1] my dagger; and Gwenhwyvar, my wife. By the truth of Heaven, thou shalt have it cheerfully, name what thou wilt." " I would that thou bless[2] my hair." " That shalt be granted thee."

And Arthur took a golden comb, and scissors, whereof the loops were of silver, and he combed his hair. And Arthur enquired of him who he was. " For my heart warms unto thee, and I know that thou art come of my blood. Tell me, therefore, who thou art." " I will tell thee," said the youth, " I am Kilhwch, the son of Kilydd, the son of Prince Kelyddon, by Goleuddydd, my mother, the daughter of Prince Anlawdd." " That is true," said Arthur. " Thou art my cousin. Whatsoever boon thou mayest ask, thou shalt receive, be it what it may that thy tongue shall name." " Pledge the truth of Heaven and the faith of thy kingdom thereof." " I pledge it thee, gladly." " I crave of thee then, that thou obtain for me Olwen, the daughter of Yspadd-

---

[1] Carnwenhan.   [2] Dress,

aden Penkawr, and this boon I likewise seek at the hands of thy warriors. I seek it from Kai, and Bedwyr, and Greidawl Galldonyd,[1] and Gwythyr the son of Greidawl, and Greid the son of Eri, and Kynddelig Kyvarwydd, and Tathal Twyll Goleu, and Maelwys the son of Baeddan, and Crychwr[2] the son of Nes, and Cubert the son of Daere, and Percos the son of Poch, and Lluber Beuthach, and Corvil Bervach, and Gwynn the son of Nudd, and Edeyrn the son of Nudd, and Gadwy[3] the son of Geraint, and Prince Fflewddur Fflam, and Ruawn Pebyr the son of Dorath, and Bradwen the son of Moren Mynawc, and Moren Mynawc himself, and Dalldav the son of Kimin Côv, and the son of Alun Dyved, and the son of Saidi, and the son of Gwryon, and Uchtryd Ardywad Kad, and Kynwas Curvagyl, and Gwrhyr Gwarthegvras, and Isperyr Ewingath, and Gallcoyt Govynynat, and Duach, and Grathach, and Nerthach, the sons of Gwawrddur Kyrvach, (these men came forth from the confines of Hell), and Kilydd Canhastyr, and Canastyr Kanllaw, and Cors Cant-Ewin, and Esgeir Gulhwch Govynkawn, and Drustwrn Hayarn, and Glewlwyd Gavaelvawr, and Lloch Llawwynnyawc, and Aunwas[4] Adeiniawc, and Sin-noch the son of Seithved, and Gwennwynwyn the son of Naw, and Bedyw the son of Seithved, and Gobrwy the son of Echel Vorddwyttwll, and Echel Vordd-wyttwll himself, and Mael the son of Roycol, and Dadweir Dallpenn, and Garwyli the son of Gwythawc Gwyr, and Gwythawc Gwyr himself, and Gormant the son of Ricca, and Menw the son of Teirgwaedd, and Digon the son of Alar, and Selyf the son of Smoit,[5] and Gusg the son of Atheu, and Nerth the

---

[1] Galldovydd.   [2] Cnychwr.   [3] And Adwy.
    [4] Annwas.   [5] Sinoit.

son of Kedarn, and Drudwas the son of Tryffin, and
Twrch the son of Perif, and Twrch the son of
Annwas, and Iona king of France, and Sel the son
of Selgi, and Teregud the son of Iaen, and Sulyen
the son of Iaen, and Bradwen the son of Iaen, and
Moren the son of Iaen, and Siawn the son of Iaen,
and Cradawc the son of Iaen. (They were men of
Caerdathal, of Arthur's kindred on his father's side.)
Dirmyg the son of Kaw, and Justic the son of Kaw,
and Etmic the son of Kaw, and Anghawd the son of
Kaw, and Ovan the son of Kaw, and Kelin the son
of Kaw, and Connyn the son of Kaw, and Mabsant
the son of Kaw, and Gwyngad the son of Kaw, and
Llwybyr the son of Kaw, and Coth the son of Kaw,
and Meilic the son of Kaw, and Kynwas the son of
Kaw, and Ardwyad the son of Kaw, and Ergyryad
the son of Kaw, and Neb the son of Kaw, and Gilda
the son of Kaw, and Calcas the son of Kaw, and
Hueil the son of Kaw, (he never yet made a request
at the hand of any Lord). And Samson Vinsych,
and Taliesin the chief of the bards, and Mamawyddan
the son of Llyr, and Llary the son of Prince Kasnar,
and Ysperni [1] the son of Fflergant king of Armorica,
and Saranhon the son of Glythwyr, and Llawr Eilerw,
and Annyanniawc the son of Menw the son of
Teirgwaedd, and Gwynn the son of Nwyvre, and
Fflam the son of Nwyvre, and Geraint the son of
Erbin, and Ermid [2] the son of Erbin, and Dyvel the
son of Erbin, and Gwynn the son of Ermid, and
Kyndrwyn the son of Ermid, and Hyveidd Unllenn,
and Eiddon Vawr Vrydic, and Reidwn Arwy, and
Gormant the son of Ricca (Arthur's brother by his
mother's side; the Penhynev of Cornwall was his
father), and Llawnrodded Varvawc, and Nodawl

[1] Ysperin.   [2] Erinit.

Varyf Twrch, and Berth the son of Kado, and
Rheidwn the son of Beli, and Iscovan Hael, and
Iscawin the son of Panon, and Morvran the son of
Tegid (no one struck him in the battle of Camlan by
reason of his ugliness ; all thought he was an
auxiliary devil. Hair had he upon him like the hair
of a stag). And Sandde Bryd Angel (no one touched
him with a spear in the battle of Camlan because of
his beauty ; all thought he was a ministering angel).
And Kynwyl Sant, the third man that escaped from
the battle of Camlan, (and he was the last who parted
from Arthur on Hengroen his horse). And Uchtryd
the son of Erim, and Eus the son of Erim, and
Henwas Adeinawg the son of Erim, and Henbedestyr
the son of Erim, and Sgilti Yscawndroed son of Erim.
(Unto these three men belonged these three qualities,
—with Henbedestyr there was not any one who
could keep pace, either on horseback or on foot :
with Henwas Adeinawg, no four-footed beast could
run the distance of an acre, much less could it go
beyond it ; and as to Sgilti Yscawndroed, when he
intended to go upon a message for his Lord, he never
sought to find a path, but knowing whither he was
to go, if his way lay through a wood he went along
the tops of the trees. During his whole life, a blade
of reed grass bent not beneath his feet, much less did
one ever break, so lightly did he tread.) Teithi Hen
the son of Gwynhan, (his dominions were swallowed
up by the sea and he himself hardly escaped, and he
came to Arthur ; and his knife had this peculiarity,
that from the time that he came there, no haft would
ever remain upon it, and owing to this a sickness
came over him, and he pined away during the
remainder of his life, and of this he died). And
Carneddyr the son of Govynyon Hen, and Gwen-

wynwyn the son of Nav Gyssevin, Arthur's champion,
and Llysgadrudd Emys, and Gwrbothu Hên, (uncles
unto Arthur were they, his mother's brothers).   Kulva-
nawyd the son of Goryon, and Llenlleawg [1] Wyddel
from the headland of Ganion, and Dyvynwal Moel,
and Dunard king of the North, Teirnon Twryf Bliant,
and Tegvan Gloff, and Tegyr Talgellawg, Gwrdinal [2]
the son of Ebrei, and Morgant Hael, Gwystyl the
son of Rhun the son of Nwython, and Llwyddeu,
the son of Nwython, and Gwydre the son of Llwyddeu,
(Gwenabwy the daughter of [Kaw] was his mother,
Hueil his uncle stabbed him, and hatred was between
Hueil and Arthur because of the wound).   Drem
the son of Dremidyd, (when the gnat arose in the
morning with the sun, he could see it from Gelli Wic
in Cornwall, as far off as Pen Blathaon in North
Britain).   And Eidyol the son of Ner, and Glwyddyn
Saer, (who constructed Ehangwen, Arthur's Hall).
Kynyr Keinvarvawc, (when he was told he had a
son born,[3] he said to his wife, ' Damsel, if thy son be
mine, his heart will be always cold, and there will
be no warmth in his hands ; and he will have another
peculiarity, if he is my son he will always be stubborn ;
and he will have another peculiarity, when he carries
a burden, whether it be large or small, no one will
be able to see it, either before him or at his back ;
and he will have another peculiarity, no one will be
able to resist water and fire so well as he will ; and
he will have another peculiarity, there will never be
a servant or an officer equal to him ').   Henwas, and
Henwyneb, (an old companion to Arthur).   Gwall-
goyc, (another ; when he came to a town, though there
were three hundred houses in it, if he wanted any

[1] Llenuleawc.   [2] Gwrdival.
[3] Kai was said to be his son.

thing, he would not let sleep come to the eyes of any-
one whilst he remained there). Berwyn the son of
Gerenhir, and Paris king of France,[1] and Osla
Gyllellvawr, (who bore a short broad dagger. When
Arthur and his hosts came before a torrent, they
would seek for a narrow place where they might pass
the water, and would lay the sheathed dagger across
the torrent, and it would form a bridge sufficient for
the armies of the three Islands of Britain, and of the
three Islands adjacent, with their spoil). Gwyddawg
the son of Menestyr, (who slew Kai, and whom
Arthur slew together with his brothers, to revenge
Kai). Garanwyn the son of Kai, and Amren the son
of Bedwyr, and Ely Amyr, and Rheu Rhwyd Dyrys,
and Rhun Rhudwern, and Eli, and Trachmyr,
(Arthur's chief huntsmen). And Llwyddeu the son
of Kelcoed, and Hunabwy the son of Gwryon, and
Gwynn Godyvron, and Gweir Datharwenniddawg,
and Gweir the son of Cadell the son of Talaryant,[2]
and Gweir Gwrhyd Ennwir, and Gweir Paladyr Hir,
(the uncles of Arthur, the brothers of his mother).
The sons of Llwch Llawwynnyawg, (from beyond the
raging sea). Lienlleawg Wyddel, and Ardderchawg
Prydain. Cas the son of Saidi, Gwrvan Gwallt
Avwyn, and Gwyilennhin the king of France, and
Gwittart the son of Oedd king of Ireland, Garseiit
Wyddel, Panawr Pen Bagad, and Ffleudor the son of
Nav, Gwynnhyvar mayor of Cornwall and Devon,
(the ninth man that rallied the battle of Camlan).
Keli and Kueli, and Gilla Coes Hydd, (he would
clear three hundred acres at one bound. The chief
leaper of Ireland was he). Sol, and Gwadyn Ossol

[1] Add. "And from him is Paris named."
[2] Gweir, son of Cadellin Talaryant (Cadellin of the silver brow).

and Gwadyn Odyeith. (Sol could stand all day upon
one foot. Gwadyn Ossol, if he stood upon the top
of the highest mountain in the world, it would
become a level plain under his feet. Gwadyn
Odyeith, the soles of his feet emitted sparks of fire
when they struck upon things hard, like the heated
mass when drawn out of the forge. He cleared the
way for Arthur when he came to any stoppage.)
Hirerwm and Hiratrwm. (The day they went on a
visit three Cantrevs provided for their entertainment,
and they feasted until noon and drank until night,
when they went to sleep. And then they devoured
the heads of the vermin through hunger, as if they
had never eaten anything. When they made a visit,
they left neither the fat nor the lean, neither the hot
nor the cold, the sour nor the sweet, the fresh nor
the salt, the boiled nor the raw.) Huarwar the son
of Aflawn, (who asked Arthur such a boon as would
satisfy him. It was the third great plague of Cornwall
when he received it. None could get a smile from
him but when he was satisfied). Gware Gwallt
Euryn. The two cubs of Gast Rhymi, Gwyddrud
and Gwyddneu Astrus. Sugyn the son of Sugnedydd,
(who would suck up the sea on which were three
hundred ships, so as to leave nothing but a dry strand.
He was broad-chested).[1] Rhacymwri, the attendant
of Arthur ; (whatever barn he was shown, were there
the produce of thirty ploughs within it, he would
strike it with an iron flail until the rafters, the beams,
and the boards, were no better than the small oats in
the mow upon the floor of the barn). Dygyflwng,
and Anoeth Veidawg. And Hir Eiddyl, and Hir
Amreu, (they were two attendants of Arthur). And
Gwevyl the son of Gwestad, (on the day that he was

[1] His flat breast was ruddy.

sad, he would let one of his lips drop below his waist, while he turned up the other like a cap upon his head). Uchtryd Varyf Draws, (who spread his red untrimmed beard over the eight-and-forty rafters which were in Arthur's Hall). Elidyr Gyvarwydd, Yskyrdav, and Yscudydd, (two attendants of Gwenhwyvar were they. Their feet were swift as their thoughts when bearing a message). Brys the son of Bryssethach, (from the Hill of the Black Fernbrake in North Britain). And Grudlwyn Gorr. Bwlch, and Kyfwlch, and Sefwlch, the sons of Cleddyf Kyfwlch, the grandsons of Cleddyf Difwlch. (Their three shields were three gleaming glitterers ; their three spears were three pointed piercers ; their three swords were three griding gashers ; Glas, Glessic, and Gleisad. Their three dogs, Call, Cuall, and Cavall. Their three horses, Hwyrdyddwd, and Drwgdyddwd, and Llwyrdyddwg.[1] Their three wives, Och, and Garym, and Diaspad. Their three grand-children, Lluched, and Neved, and Eissiwed. Their three daughters, Drwg, and Gwaeth, and Gwaethav Oll. Their three handmaids, Eheubryd the daughter of Kyfwlch, Gorascwrn the daughter of Nerth, Ewaedan the daughter of Kynvelyn Keudawd Pwyll the half man.) Dwnn Diessic Unbenn, Eiladyr the son of Pen Llarcau, Kynedyr Wyllt the son of Hettwn Talaryant, Sawyl, Ben Uchel, Gwalchmai the son of Gwyar, Gwalhaved the son of Gwyar, Gwrhyr Gwastawd Ieithoedd, (to whom all tongues were known,) and Kethcrwn[2] the Priest. Clust the son of Clustveinad, (though he were buried seven cubits beneath the earth, he would hear the ant, fifty miles off, rise from her nest in the morning). Medyr the

[1] Hwyrdyddwc, Drwgdyddwc, and Llwyrdyddwc.
[2] Cethtrwm.

son of Methredydd, (from Gelli Wic he could, in a twinkling, shoot the wren through the two legs upon Esgeir Oervel in Ireland). Gwiawn Llygad Cath, (who would cut a haw from the eye of the gnat without hurting him). Ol the son of Olwydd; (seven years before he was born his father's swine were carried off, and when he grew up a man, he tracked the swine, and brought them back in seven herds). Bedwini the Bishop, (who blessed Arthur's meat and drink). For the sake of the golden-chained daughters of this island. For the sake of Gwenhwyvar, its chief lady, and Gwennhwyach her sister, and Rathtyeu the only daughter of Clemenhill, and Rhelemon the daughter of Kai, and Tannwen the daughter of Gweir Datharweniddawg.[1] Gwenn Alarch, the daughter of Kynwyl Canbwch.[2] Eurneid the daughter of Clydno Eiddin. Eneuawc the daughter of Bedwyr. Enrydreg the daughter of Tudvathar. Gwennwledyr the daughter of Gwaledyr Kyrvach. Erddudnid the daughter of Tryffin. Eurolwen the daughter of Gwdolwyn Gorr. Teleri the daughter of Peul. Indeg the daughter of Garwy[3] Hir. Morvudd the daughter of Urien Rheged. Gwenllian Deg the majestic maiden. Creiddylad the daughter of Llud Llaw Ereint. (She was the most splendid maiden in the three Islands of the mighty, and in the three Islands adjacent, and for her Gwythyr the son of Greidawl and Gwynn the son of Nudd fight every first of May until the day of doom.) Ellylw the daughter of Neol Kynn-Crog. (She lived three ages.) Essyllt Vinwen, and Essyllt Vingul." And all these did Kilhwch son of Kilydd adjure to obtain his boon.

Then said Arthur, "Oh! Chieftain, I have never heard of the maiden of whom thou speakest, nor of

[1] Gweirdathar Wenidawc.   [2] Canhwch.   [3] Arwy.

her kindred, but I will gladly send messengers in
search of her. Give me time to seek her." And the
youth said, "I will willingly grant from this night to
that at the end of the year to do so." Then Arthur
sent messengers to every land within his dominions,
to seek for the maiden, and at the end of the year
Arthur's messengers returned without having gained
any knowledge or intelligence concerning Olwen,
more than on the first day. Then said Kilhwch,
"Every one has received his boon, and I yet lack
mine. I will depart and bear away thy honour with
me." Then said Kai, "Rash chieftain! dost thou
reproach Arthur? Go with us, and we will not part
until thou dost either confess that the maiden exists
not in the world, or until we obtain her." Thereupon
Kai rose up. Kai had this peculiarity, that his breath
lasted nine nights and nine days under water, and he
could exist nine nights and nine days without sleep.
A wound from Kai's sword no physician could heal.
Very subtle was Kai. When it pleased him he could
render himself as tall as the highest tree in the forest.
And he had another peculiarity,—so great was the
heat of his nature, that when it rained hardest, whatever he carried remained dry for a handbreadth above
and a handbreadth below his hand; and when his
companions were coldest, it was to them as fuel with
which to light their fire.

And Arthur called Bedwyr, who never shrank from
any enterprise upon which Kai was bound. None
were equal to him in swiftness throughout this Island
except Arthur and Drych Ail Kibddar. And although
he was one-handed, three warriors could not shed
blood faster than he on the field of battle. Another
property he had, his lance would produce a wound
equal to those of nine opposing lances.

And Arthur called to Kynddelig the Guide, "Go thou upon this expedition with the chieftain." For as good a guide was he in a land which he had never seen as he was in his own.

He called Gwrhyr Gwalstawt Ieithoedd, because he knew all tongues.

He called Gwalchmai the son of Gwyar, because he never returned home without achieving the adventure of which he went in quest. He was the best of footmen and the best of knights. He was nephew to Arthur, the son of his sister, and his cousin.

And Arthur called Menw the son of Teirgwaedd, in order that if they went into a savage country, he might cast a charm and an illusion over them, so that none might see them, whilst they could see every one.

They journeyed until they came to a vast open plain, wherein they saw a great castle, which was the fairest of the castles of the world. And they journeyed that day until the evening, and when they thought they were nigh to the castle, they were no nearer to it than they had been in the morning. And the second and the third day they journeyed, and even then scarcely could they reach so far. And when they came before the castle, they beheld a vast flock of sheep, which was boundless, and without an end. And upon the top of a mound there was a herdsman, keeping the sheep. And a rug made of skins was upon him; and by his side was a shaggy mastiff, larger than a steed nine winters old. Never had he lost even a lamb from his flock, much less a large sheep. He let no occasion ever pass without doing some hurt and harm. All the dead trees and bushes in the plain he burnt with his breath down to the very ground.

Then said Kai, "Gwrhyr Gwalstawt Ieithoedd,

go thou and salute yonder man." "Kai," said he,
" I engaged not to go further than thou thyself."
"Let us go then together," answered Kai.[1]   Said
Menw the son of Teirgwaedd, " Fear not to go thither,
for I will cast a spell upon the dog, so that he shall
injure no one."   And they went up to the mound
whereon the herdsman was, and they said to him,
" How dost thou fare? O herdsman ! "   "No less
fair be it to you than to me."   " Truly, art thou the
chief?"   "There is no hurt to injure me but my
own."[2]   " Whose are the sheep that thou dost keep,
and to whom does yonder castle belong ? "   " Stupid
are ye, truly !   Through the whole world is it known
that this is the castle of Yspaddaden Penkawr."
" And who art thou ? "   " I am called Custennin the
son of Dyfnedig, and my brother Yspaddaden Penkawr
oppressed me because of my possession.   And ye
also, who are ye ? "   " We are an embassy from
Arthur, come to seek Olwen, the daughter of
Yspaddaden Penkawr."   "Oh men ! the mercy of
Heaven be upon you, do not that for all the world.
None who ever came hither on this quest has returned
alive."   And the herdsman rose up.   And as he
arose, Kilhwch gave unto him a ring of gold.   And
he sought to put on the ring, but it was too small for
him, so he placed it in the finger of his glove.   And
he went home, and gave the glove to his spouse to
keep.   And she took the ring from the glove when it
was given her, and she said, " Whence came this ring,
for thou art not wont to have good fortune ? "   " I
went," said he, " to the sea to seek for fish, and lo, I
saw a corpse borne by the waves.   And a fairer corpse

---

[1] " We all of us will come there," said Kai.
[2] This dialogue consists of a series of repartees, with a play
upon words which it is impossible to follow in the translation.

F

than it did I never behold. And from its finger did
I take this ring." "Oh man! does the sea permit its
dead to wear jewels? Show me then this body."
" Oh wife, him to whom this ring belonged thou shalt
see here in the evening."[1] "And who is he?" asked
the woman." "Kilhwch the son of Kilydd, the son
of Prince Kelyddon, by Goleuddydd 'the daughter of
Prince Anlawdd, his mother, who is come to seek
Olwen as his wife." And when she heard that, her
feelings were divided between the joy that she had
that her nephew, the son of her sister, was coming to
her, and sorrow because she had never known any
one depart alive who had come on that quest.

And they went forward to the gate of Custennin
the herdsman's dwelling. And when she heard their
footsteps approaching, she ran out with joy to meet
them. And Kai snatched a billet out of the pile.
And when she met them she sought to throw her arms
about their necks. And Kai placed the log between
her two hands, and she squeezed it so that it became
a twisted coil. "Oh woman," said Kai, "if thou
hadst squeezed me thus, none could ever again have
set their affections on me. Evil love were this."
They entered into the house, and were served; and
soon after they all went forth to amuse themselves.
Then the woman opened a stone chest that was
before the chimney corner, and out of it arose a
youth with yellow curling hair. Said Gwrhyr, "It is
a pity to hide this youth. I know that it is not his
own crime that is thus visited upon him." "This is
but a remnant," said the woman. "Three and
twenty of my sons has Yspaddaden Penkawr slain,

---

[1] " Oh man, since the sea does not allow a beautiful dead man
in it, show me that dead body." " Oh woman, the one to
whom the dead body belongs thou wilt see here this evening."

and I have no more hope of this one than of the others." Then said Kai, "Let him come and be a companion with me, and he shall not be slain unless I also am slain with him." And they ate. And the woman asked them, "Upon what errand come you here?" "We come to seek Olwen for this youth." Then said the woman, "In the name of Heaven, since no one from the castle hath yet seen you, return again whence you came." "Heaven is our witness, that we will not return until we have seen the maiden." Said Kai, "Does she ever come hither, so that she may be seen?" "She comes here every Saturday to wash her head, and in the vessel where she washes, she leaves all her rings, and she never either comes herself or sends any messengers to fetch them." "Will she come here if she is sent to?" "Heaven knows that I will not destroy my soul, nor will I betray those that trust me; unless you will pledge me your faith that you will not harm her, I will not send to her." "We pledge it," said they. So a message was sent, and she came.

The maiden was clothed in a robe of flame-coloured silk, and about her neck was a collar of ruddy gold, on which were precious emeralds and rubies. More yellow was her head than the flower of the broom, and her skin was whiter than the foam of the wave, and fairer were her hands and her fingers than the blossoms of the wood anemone amidst the spray of the meadow fountain. The eye of the trained hawk, the glance of the three-mewed falcon, was not brighter than hers. Her bosom was more snowy than the breast of the white swan, her cheek was redder than the reddest roses. Whoso beheld her was filled with her love. Four white trefoils sprung up wherever she trod. And therefore was she called Olwen.

She entered the house, and sat beside Kilhwch upon the foremost bench ; and as soon as he saw her he knew her. And Kilhwch said unto her, "Ah ! maiden, thou art she whom I have loved; come away with me lest they speak evil of thee and of me. Many a day have I loved thee." "I cannot do this, for I have pledged my faith to my father not to go without his counsel, for his life will last only until the time of my espousals. Whatever is, must be. But I will give thee advice if thou wilt take it. Go, ask me of my father, and that which he shall require of thee, grant it, and thou wilt obtain me ; but if thou deny him anything, thou wilt not obtain me, and it will be well for thee if thou escape with thy life." "I promise all this, if occasion offer," said he.[1]

She returned to her chamber, and they all rose up and followed her to the castle. And they slew the nine porters that were at the nine gates in silence. And they slew the nine watch-dogs without one of them barking. And they went forward to the hall.

"The greeting of Heaven and of man be unto thee, Yspaddaden Penkawr," said they. "And you, wherefore come you?" "We come to ask thy daughter Olwen, for Kilhwch the son of Kilydd, the son of Prince Kelyddon." "Where are my pages and my servants?[2] Raise up the forks beneath my two eyebrows which have fallen over my eyes, that I may see the fashion of my son-in-law." And they did so. "Come hither to-morrow, and you shall have an answer.

They rose to go forth, and Yspaddaden Penkawr seized one of the three poisoned darts that lay beside him, and threw it after them. And Bedwyr caught

---

[1] " I promise all this, and will obtain it," said he.
[2] " Where are my bad servants and my knaves?"

it, and flung it, and pierced Yspaddaden Penkawr grievously with it through the knee.[1] Then he said, "A cursed ungentle son-in-law, truly. I shall ever walk the worse for his rudeness, and shall ever be without a cure. This poisoned iron pains me like the bite of a gad-fly. Cursed be the smith who forged it, and the anvil whereon it was wrought! So sharp is it!"

That night also they took up their abode in the house of Custennin the herdsman. The next day with the dawn, they arrayed themselves in haste, and proceeded to the castle, and entered the hall, and they said, "Yspaddaden Penkawr, give us thy daughter in consideration of her dower and her maiden fee, which we will pay to thee and to her two kinswomen likewise. And unless thou wilt do so, thou shalt meet with thy death on her account." Then he said, "Her four great-grandmothers, and her four great-grandsires are yet alive, it is needful that I take counsel of them." "Be it so," answered they, "we will go to meat." As they rose up; he took the second dart that was beside him, and cast it after them. And Menw the son of Gwaedd caught it, and flung it back at him, and wounded him in the centre of the breast, so that it came out at the small of his back. "A cursed ungentle son-in-law, truly," said he, "the hard iron pains me like the bite of a horse-leech. Cursed be the hearth whereon it was heated, and the smith who formed it! So sharp is it! Henceforth, whenever I go up a hill, I shall have a scant in my breath, and a pain in my chest, and I shall often loathe my food." And they went to meat.

And the third day they returned to the palace

[1] Knee-pan.

And Yspaddaden Penkawr said to them, "Shoot not at me again unless you desire death. Where are my attendants? Lift up the forks of my eyebrows which have fallen over my eyeballs, that I may see the fashion of my son-in-law." Then they arose, and, as they did so, Yspaddaden Penkawr took the third poisoned dart, and cast it at them. And Kilhwch caught it, and threw it vigorously, and wounded him through the eyeball, so that the dart came out at the back of his head. "A cursed ungentle son-in-law, truly! As long as I remain alive, my eyesight will be the worse. Whenever I go against the wind, my eyes will water; and peradventure my head will burn, and I shall have a giddiness every new moon. Cursed be the fire in which it was forged. Like the bite of a mad dog is the stroke of this poisoned iron." And they went to meat.

And the next day they came again to the palace, and they said, "Shoot not at us any more, unless thou desirest such hurt, and harm, and torture as thou now hast, and even more. Give me thy daughter; and if thou wilt not give her, thou shalt receive thy death because of her." "Where is he that seeks my daughter? Come hither where I may see thee." And they placed him a chair face to face with him.

Said Yspaddaden Penkawr, "Is it thou that seekest my daughter?" "It is I," answered Kilhwch. "I must have thy pledge that thou wilt not do towards me otherwise than is just, and, when I have gotten that which I shall name, my daughter thou shalt have." "I promise thee that willingly," said Kilhwch; "name what thou wilt." "I will do so," said he.

"Seest thou yonder vast hill?" "I see it." "I

require that it be rooted up, and that the grubbings
be burned for manure on the face of the land, and
that it be ploughed and sown in one day, and in one
day that the grain ripen.   And of that wheat I intend
to make food and liquor fit for the wedding of thee
and my daughter.   And all this I require to be done
in one day."

"It will be easy for me to compass this, although
thou mayest think that it will not be easy."

"Though this be easy for thee, there is yet that
which will not be so.   No husbandman can till or
prepare this land, so wild is it, except Amaethon the
son of Don, and he will not come with thee by his
own free will, and thou wilt not be able to compel
him."

"It will be easy for me to compass this, although
thou mayest think that it will not be easy."

"Though thou get this, there is yet that which
thou wilt not get.   Govannon the son of Don to
come to the headland to rid the iron, he will do no
work of his own good will except for a lawful king,
and thou wilt not be able to compel him."

"It will be easy for me to compass this."

"Though thou get this, there is yet that which
thou wilt not get; the two dun oxen of Gwlwlyd,[1]
both yoked together, to plough the wild land yonder
stoutly.   He will not give them of his own free will,
and thou wilt not be able to compel him."

"It will be easy for me to compass this."

"Though thou get this, there is yet that which thou
wilt not get; the yellow and the brindled bull yoked
together do I require."

"It will be easy for me to compass this."

"Though thou get this, there is yet that which thou

---

[1] The two oxen of Gwlwlwyd Wineu.

wilt not get; the two horned oxen, one of which is beyond, and the other this side of the peaked mountain, yoked together in the same plough. And these are Nynniaw and Peibaw, whom God turned into oxen on account of their sins."

"It will be easy for me to compass this."

"Though thou get this, there is yet that which thou wilt not get. Seest thou yonder red tilled ground?"

"I see it."

"When first I met the mother of this maiden, nine bushels of flax were sown therein, and none has yet sprung up, neither white nor black; and I have the measure by me still. I require to have the flax to sow in the new land yonder, that when it grows up it may make a white wimple, for my daughter's head on the day of thy wedding."

"It will be easy for me to compass this, although thou mayest think that it will not be easy."

"Though thou get this, there is yet that which thou wilt not get. Honey that is nine times sweeter than the honey of the virgin swarm, without scum and bees, do I require to make bragget for the feast."

"It will be easy for me to compass this, although thou mayest think that it will not be easy."

"The vessel of Llwyr the son of Llwyryon, which is of the utmost value. There is no other vessel in the world that can hold this drink. Of his free will thou wilt not get it, and thou canst not compel him."

"It will be easy for me to compass this, although thou mayest think that it will not be easy."

"Though thou get this, there is yet that which thou wilt not get. The basket of Gwyddneu Garanhir, if the whole world should come together, thrice nine men at a time, the meat that each of them desired would be found within it. I require to eat therefrom on the night that my daughter becomes thy bride. He will give it to no one of his own free will, and thou canst not compel him."

"It will be easy for me to compass this, although thou mayest think that it will not be easy."

"Though thou get this, there is yet that which thou wilt not get. The horn of Gwlgawd Gododin to serve us with liquor that night. He will not give it of his own free will, and thou wilt not be able to compel him."

"It will be easy for me to compass this, although thou mayest think that it will not be easy."

"Though thou get this, there is yet that which thou wilt not get. The harp of Teirtu to play to us that night.[1] When a man desires that it should play, it does so of itself, and when he desires that it should cease, it ceases. And this he will not give of his own free will, and thou wilt not be able to compel him."

"It will be easy for me to compass this, although thou mayest think that it will not be easy."

"Though thou get this, there is yet that which thou wilt not get. The cauldron of Diwrnach Wyddel, the steward of Odgar the son of Aedd, king of Ireland, to boil the meat for thy marriage feast."

"It will be easy for me to compass this, although thou mayest think that it will not be easy."

"Though thou get this, there is yet that which thou wilt not get. It is needful for me to wash my head, and shave my beard, and I require the tusk of Yskithyrwyn Benbaedd to shave myself withal, neither shall I profit by its use if it be not plucked alive out of his head."

"It will be easy for me to compass this, although thou mayest think that it will not be easy."

[1] The harp of Teirtu to console me that night.

"Though thou get this, there is yet that which thou wilt not get. There is no one in the world that can pluck it out of his head except Odgar the son of Aedd, king of Ireland."

"It will be easy for me to compass this."

"Though thou get this, there is yet that which thou wilt not get. I will not trust any one to keep the tusk except Gado of North Britain. Now the threescore Cantrevs of North Britain are under his sway, and of his own free will he will not come out of his kingdom, and thou wilt not be able to compel him."

"It will be easy for me to compass this, although thou mayest think that it wilt not be easy."

"Though thou get this, there is yet that which thou wilt not get. I must spread out my hair in order to shave it, and it will never be spread out unless I have the blood of the jet black sorceress, the daughter of the pure white sorceress, from Pen Nant Govid, on the confines of Hell."

"It will be easy for me to compass this, although thou mayest think that it will not be easy."

"Though thou get this, there is yet that which thou wilt not get. I will not have the blood unless I have it warm, and no vessels will keep warm the liquid that is put therein except the bottles of Gwyddolwyn Gorr, which preserve the heat of the liquor that is put into them in the east, until they arrive at the west. And he will not give them of his own free will, and thou wilt not be able to compel him."

"It will be easy for me to compass this, although thou mayest think that it will not be easy."

"Though thou get this, there is yet that which thou wilt not get. Some will desire fresh milk, and it will not be possible to have fresh milk for all, unless we have the bottles of Rhinnon Rhin Barnawd, wherein no liquor ever turns sour. And he will not give them of his own free will, and thou wilt not be able to compel him."

"It will be easy for me to compass this, although thou mayest think that it will not be easy."

"Though thou get this, there is yet that which thou wilt not get. Throughout the world there is not a comb or scissors with which I can arrange my hair, on account of its rankness, except the comb and scissors that are between the two ears of Twrch Trwyth, the son of Prince Tared. He will not give them of his own free will, and thou wilt not be able to compel him."

"It will be easy for me to compass this, although thou mayest think that it will not be easy."

"Though thou get this, there is yet that which thou wilt not get. It will not be possible to hunt Twrch Trwyth without Drudwyn, the whelp of Greid, the son of Eri."

"It will be easy for me to compass this, although thou mayest think that it will not be easy."

"Though thou get this, there is yet that which thou wilt not get. Throughout the world there is not a leash that can hold him, except the leash of Cwrs Cant Ewin."

"It will be easy for me to compass this, although thou mayest think that it will not be easy."

"Though thou get this, there is yet that which thou wilt not get. Throughout the world there is no collar that wilt hold the leash except the collar of Canhastyr Canllaw."

"It will be easy for me to compass this, although thou mayest think that it will not be easy."

"Though thou get this, there is yet that which thou

wilt not get. The chain of Kilydd Canhastyr to fasten the collar to the leash."

"It will be easy for me to compass this, although thou mayest think that it will not be easy."

"Though thou get this, there is yet that which thou wilt not get. Throughout the world there is not a huntsman who can hunt with this dog, except Mabon the son of Modron. He was taken from his mother when three nights old, and it is not known where he now is, nor whether he is living or dead."

"It will be easy for me to compass this, although thou mayest think that it will not be easy."

"Though thou get this, there is yet that which thou wilt not get. Gwynn Mygdwn, the horse of Gweddw that is as swift as the wave, to carry Mabon the son of Modron to hunt the Boar Trwyth. He will not give him of his own free will, and thou wilt not be able to compel him."

"It will be easy for me to compass this, although thou mayest think that it will not be easy."

"Though thou get this, there is yet that which thou wilt not get. Thou wilt not get Mabon, for it is not known where he is, unless thou find Eidoel, his kinsman in blood, the son of Aer. For it would be useless to seek for him. He is his cousin."

"It will be easy for me to compass this, although thou mayest think that it will not be easy."

"Though thou get this, there is yet that which thou wilt not get. Garselit the Gwyddelian[1] is the chief huntsman of Ireland; the Twrch Trwyth can never be hunted without him."

"It will be easy for me to compass this, although thou mayest think that it will not be easy."

"Though thou get this, there is yet that which thou

[1] Garselit Wyddel.

wilt not get. A leash made from the beard of Dissull Varvawc, for that is the only one that can hold those two cubs. And the leash will be of no avail unless it be plucked from his beard while he is alive, and twitched out with wooden tweezers. While he lives he will not suffer this to be done to him, and the leash will be of no use should he be dead, because it will be brittle."

" It will be easy for me to compass this, although thou mayest think that it will not be easy."

" Though thou get this, there is yet that which thou wilt not get. Throughout the world there is no huntsman that can hold those two whelps, except Kynedyr Wyllt, the son of Hettwn Glafyrawc ; he is nine times more wild than the wildest beast upon the mountains. Him wilt thou never get, neither wilt thou ever get my daughter."

" It will be easy for me to compass this, although thou mayest think that it will not be easy."

" Though thou get this, there is yet that which thou wilt not get. It is not possible to hunt the Boar Trwyth without Gwynn the son of Nudd, whom God has placed over the brood of devils in Annwn, lest they should destroy the present race. He will never be spared thence."

" It will be easy for me to compass this, although thou mayest think that it will not be easy."

" Though thou get this, there is yet that which thou wilt not get. There is not a horse in the world that can carry Gwynn to hunt the Twrch Trwyth, except Du, the horse of Mor of Oerveddawg." [1]

" It will be easy for me to compass this, although thou mayest think that it will not be easy."

" Though thou get this, there is yet that which thou

[1] Moro Oerveddawc.

wilt not get. Until Gilennhin the king of France shall come, the Twrch Trwyth cannot be hunted. It will be unseemly for him to leave his kingdom for thy sake, and he will never come hither."

"It will be easy for me to compass this, although thou mayest think that it will not be easy."

"Though thou get this, there is yet that which thou wilt not get. The Twrch Trwyth can never be hunted without the son of Alun Dyved; he is well skilled in letting loose the dogs."

"It will be easy for me to compass this, although thou mayest think that it will not be easy."

"Though thou get this, there is yet that which thou wilt not get. The Twrch Trwyth cannot be hunted unless thou get Aned and Aethlem. They are as swift as the gale of wind, and they were never let loose upon a beast that they did not kill him."

"It will be easy for me to compass this, although thou mayest think that it will not be easy."

"Though thou get this, there is yet that which thou wilt not get; Arthur and his companions to hunt the Twrch Trwyth. He is a mighty man, and he will not come for thee, neither wilt thou be able to compel him."

"It will be easy for me to compass this, although thou mayest think that it will not be easy."

"Though thou get this, there is yet that which thou wilt not get. The Twrch Trwyth cannot be hunted unless thou get Bwlch, and Kyfwlch, [and Sefwlch,] the grandsons of Cleddyf Difwlch. Their three shields are three gleaming glitterers. Their three spears are three pointed piercers. Their three swords are three griding gashers, Glas, Glessic, and Clersag. Their three dogs, Call, Cuall, and Cavall. Their three horses, Hwyrdydwg, and

Drwgdydwg, and Llwyrdydwg. Their three wives, Och, and Geram, and Diaspad. Their three grandchildren, Lluched, and Vyned, and Eissiwed. Their three daughters, Drwg, and Gwaeth, and Gwaethav Oll. Their three handmaids, [Eheubryd, the daughter of Kyfwlch; Gorasgwrn, the daughter of Nerth; and Gwaedan, the daughter of Kynvelyn.] These three men shall sound the horn, and all the others shall shout, so that all will think that the sky is falling to the earth."

" It will be easy for me to compass this, although thou mayest think that it will not be easy."

" Though thou get this, there is yet that which thou wilt not get. The sword of Gwrnach the Giant; he will never be slain except therewith. Of his own free will he will not give it, either for a price or as a gift, and thou wilt never be able to compel him."

" It will be easy for me to compass this, although thou mayest think that it will not be easy."

" Though thou get this, there is yet that which thou wilt not get. Difficulties shalt thou meet with, and nights without sleep, in seeking this, and if thou obtain it not, neither shalt thou obtain my daughter."

" Horses shall I have, and chivalry; and my lord and kinsman Arthur will obtain for me all these things. And I shall gain thy daughter, and thou shalt lose thy life."

" Go forward. And thou shalt not be chargeable for food or raiment for my daughter while thou art seeking these things; and when thou hast compassed all these marvels, thou shalt have my daughter for thy wife."

All that day they journeyed until the evening, and

then they beheld a vast castle, which was the largest
in the world.   And lo, a black man, huger than three
of the men of this world, came out from the castle.
And they spoke unto him, "Whence comest thou, O
man?"   "From the castle which you see yonder."
"Whose castle is that?" asked they.   "Stupid are
ye truly, O men.   There is no one in the world that
does not know to whom this castle belongs.   It is
the castle of Gwrnach the Giant."   "What treatment
is there for guests and strangers that alight in that
castle?"   "Oh! chieftain, Heaven protect thee.
No guest ever returned thence alive, and no one
may enter therein unless he brings with him his
craft."

Then they proceeded towards the · gate.   Said
Gwrhyr Gwalstawd Ieithoedd, "Is there a porter?"
"There is.   And thou, if thy tongue be not mute in
thy head, wherefore dost thou call?"   "Open the
gate."   "I will not open it."   "Wherefore wilt thou
not?"   "The knife is in the meat, and the drink is
in the horn, and there is revelry in the hall of
Gwrnach the Giant, and except for a craftsman who
brings his craft, the gate will not be opened to-night."
"Verily, porter," then said Kai, "my craft bring I
with me."   "What is thy craft?"   "The best
burnisher of swords am I in the world."   "I will
go and tell this unto Gwrnach the Giant, and I will
bring thee an answer."

So the porter went in, and Gwrnach said to him,
"Hast thou any news from the gate?"   "I have.
There is a party at the door of the gate who desire
to come in."   "Didst thou enquire of them if they
possessed any art?"   "I did enquire," said he, "and
one told me that he was well skilled in the burnish-
ing of swords."   "We have need of him then.   For

some time have I sought for some one to polish my
sword, and could find no one. Let this man enter,
since he brings with him his craft."

The porter thereupon returned, and opened the
gate. And Kai went in by himself, and he saluted
Gwrnach the Giant. And a chair was placed for him
opposite to Gwrnach. And Gwrnach said to him,
"Oh man! is it true that is reported of thee that
thou knowest how to burnish swords?" "I know
full well how to do so," answered Kai. Then was
the sword of Gwrnach brought to him. And Kai
took a blue whetstone from under his arm, and
asked him whether he would have it burnished
white or blue. "Do with it as it seems good to thee,
and as thou wouldest if it were thine own." Then
Kai polished one half of the blade and put it in his
hand. "Will this please thee?" asked he. "I
would rather than all that is in my dominions that
the whole of it were like unto this. It is a marvel
to me that such a man as thou should be without a
companion." "Oh! noble sir, I have a companion,
albeit he is not skilled in this art." "Who may he
be?" "Let the porter go forth, and I will tell him
whereby he may know him. The head of his lance
will leave its shaft, and draw blood from the wind,
and will descend upon its shaft again." Then the
gate was opened, and Bedwyr entered. And Kai
said, "Bedwyr is very skilful, although he knows not
this art."

And there was much discourse among those who
were without, because that Kai and Bedwyr had
gone in. And a young man who was with them, the
only son of Custennin the herdsman, got in also.
And he caused all his companions to keep close to
him as he passed the three wards, and until he came

G

into the midst of the castle.[1] And his companions
said unto the son of Custennin, "Thou hast done
this! Thou art the best of all men." And thenceforth he was called Goreu, the son of Custennin.
Then they dispersed to their lodgings, that they
might slay those who lodged therein, unknown to
the Giant.

The sword was now polished, and Kai gave it unto
the hand of Gwrnach the Giant, to see if he were
pleased with his work. And the Giant said, "The
work is good, I am content therewith." Said Kai,
"It is thy scabbard that hath rusted thy sword; give
it to me that I may take out the wooden sides of it,
and put in new ones." And he took the scabbard
from him, and the sword in the other hand. And he
came and stood over against the Giant, as if he would
have put the sword into the scabbard; and with it he
struck at the head of the Giant, and cut off his head
at one blow. Then they despoiled the castle, and
took from it what goods and jewels they would. And
again on the same day, at the beginning of the year,
they came to Arthur's Court, bearing with them the
sword of Gwrnach the Giant.

Now when they had told Arthur how they had
sped, Arthur said, "Which of these marvels will it be
best for us to seek first?" "It will be best," said
they, "to seek Mabon the son of Modron; and he
will not be found unless we first find Eidoel, the son
of Aer, his kinsman." Then Arthur rose up, and the
warriors of the Islands of Britain with him, to seek for
Eidoel; and they proceeded until they came before
the Castle of Glivi,[2] where Eidoel was imprisoned.

---

[1] And what he and his companions with him did was this—
they crossed the three wards until he was within the fortress.

[2] Glini.

Glivi [1] stood on the summit of his Castle, and he said, "Arthur, what requirest thou of me, since nothing remains to me in this fortress, and I have neither joy nor pleasure in it; neither wheat nor oats? Seek not therefore to do me harm." Said Arthur, "Not to injure thee came I hither, but to seek for the prisoner that is with thee." "I will give thee my prisoner, though I had not thought to give him up to any one; and therewith shalt thou have my support and my aid."

His followers said unto Arthur, "Lord, go thou home, thou canst not proceed with thy host in quest of such small adventures as these." Then said Arthur, "It were well for thee, Gwrhyr Gwalstawd Iethoedd, to go upon this quest, for thou knowest all languages, and art familiar with [2] those of the birds and the beasts. Thou Eidoel oughtest likewise to go with my men in search of thy cousin. And as for you, Kai and Bedwyr, I have hope of whatever adventure ye are in quest of, that ye will achieve it. Achieve ye this adventure for me."

They went forward until they came to the Ousel of Cilgwri. And Gwrhyr adjured her for the sake of Heaven, saying, "Tell me if thou knowest aught of Mabon the son of Modron, who was taken when three nights old from between his mother and the wall." And the Ousel answered, "When I first came here, there was a smith's anvil in this place, and I was then a young bird; and from that time no work has been done upon it, save the pecking of my beak every evening, and now there is not so much as the size of a nut remaining thereof; yet the vengeance of Heaven be upon me, if during all that time I have ever heard of the man for whom you enquire.

[1] Glini.   [2] Add "some of."

Nevertheless I will do that which is right, and that which it is fitting that I should do for an embassy from Arthur. There is a race of animals who were formed before me, and I will be your guide to them."

So they proceeded to the place where was the Stag of Redynvre. "Stag of Redynvre, behold we are come to thee, an embassy from Arthur, for we have not heard of any animal older than thou. Say, knowest thou aught of Mabon the son of Modron, who was taken from his mother when three nights old?" The Stag said, "When first I came hither, there was a plain all around me, without any trees save one oak sapling,[1] which grew up to be an oak with an hundred branches. And that oak has since perished, so that now nothing remains of it but the withered stump; and from that day to this I have been here, yet have I never heard of the man for whom you enquire. Nevertheless, being an embassy from Arthur, I will be your guide to the place where there is an animal which was formed before I was."

So they proceeded to the place where was the Owl of Cwm Cawlwyd. "Owl of Cwm Cawlwyd, here is an embassy from Arthur; knowest thou aught of Mabon the son of Modron, who was taken after three nights from his mother?" "If I knew I would tell you. When first I came hither, the wide valley you see was a wooded glen. And a race of men came and rooted it up. And there grew there a second wood; and this wood is the third. My wings, are they not withered stumps? Yet all this time, even until to-day, I have never heard of the man for whom you enquire. Nevertheless, I will be the guide of Arthur's embassy until you come to the place where is the oldest animal

---

[1] There was but one horn on each side of my head, and there were no trees here except one oak sapling.

in this world, and the one that has travelled most, the Eagle of Gwern Abwy."

Gwrhyr said, " Eagle of Gwern Abwy, we have come to thee an embassy from Arthur, to ask thee if thou knowest aught of Mabon the son of Modron, who was taken from his mother when he was three nights old." The Eagle said, " I have been here for a great space of time, and when I first came hither there was a rock here, from the top of which I pecked at the stars every evening ; and now it is not so much as a span high. From that day to this I have been. here, and I have never heard of the man for whom you enquire, except once when I went in search of food as far as Llyn Llyw. And when I came there, I struck my talons into a salmon, thinking he would serve me as food for a long time. But he drew me into the deep, and I was scarcely able to escape from him. After that I went with my whole kindred to attack him, and to try to destroy him, but he sent messengers, and made peace with me ; and came and besought me to take fifty fish spears out of his back. Unless he know something of him whom you seek, I cannot tell who may. However, I will guide you to the place where he is."

So they went thither ; and the Eagle said, " Salmon of Llyn Llyw, I have come to thee with an embassy from Arthur, to ask thee if thou knowest aught concerning Mabon the son of Modron, who was taken away at three nights old from his mother." " As much as I know I will tell thee. With every tide I go along the river upwards, until I come near to the walls of Gloucester, and there have I found such wrong as I never found elsewhere ; and to the end that ye may give credence thereto, let one of you go thither upon each of my two shoulders." So Kai and Gwrhyr

Gwalstawd Ieithoedd went upon the two shoulders of
the salmon, and they proceeded until they came unto
the wall of the prison, and they heard a great wailing
and lamenting from the dungeon.[1] Said Gwrhyr,
" Who is it that laments in this house of stone? "
" Alas, there is reason enough for whoever is here to
lament. It is Mabon the son of Modron who is here

imprisoned; and no imprisonment was ever so
grievous as mine, neither that of Lludd Llaw Ereint,
nor that of Greid the son of Eri." " Hast thou hope
of being released for gold, or for silver, or for any
gifts of wealth, or through battle and fighting? "
" By fighting will whatever I may gain be obtained."

---

[1] And they proceeded until they came to the wall opposite to
where the prisoner was, where they heard lamentations and
groaning on the other side of the wall,

Then they went thence, and returned to Arthur, and they told him where Mabon the son of Modron was imprisoned. And Arthur summoned the warriors of the Island, and they journeyed as far as Gloucester, to the place where Mabon was in prison. Kai and Bedwyr went upon the shoulders of the fish, whilst the warriors of Arthur attacked the castle. And Kai broke through the wall into the dungeon, and brought away the prisoner upon his back, whilst the fight was going on between the warriors. And Arthur returned home, and Mabon with him at liberty.

Said Arthur, " Which of the marvels will it be best for us now to seek first ? " " It will be best to seek for the two cubs of Gast Rhymhi." " Is it known," said Arthur, " where she is ? " " She is in Aber Deu Gleddyf," said one. Then Arthur went to the house of Tringad, in Aber Cleddyf, and he enquired of him whether he had heard of her there." " In what form may she be ? " " She is in the form of a she-wolf," said he ; "and with her there are two cubs." " She has often slain my herds, and she is there below in a cave in Aber Cleddyf."

So Arthur went in his ship Prydwen by sea, and the others went by land, to hunt her. And they surrounded her and her two cubs, and God did change them again for Arthur into their own form. And the host of Arthur dispersed themselves into parties of one and two.

On a certain day, as Gwythyr the son of Greidawl was walking over a mountain, he heard a wailing and a grievous cry. And when he heard it,[1] he sprung

[1] And it was piteous to hear them. And he hastened to the place.

forward, and went towards it. And when he came
there, he drew his sword, and smote off an ant-hill
close to the earth, whereby it escaped being burned in
the fire. And the ants said to him, "Receive from us
the blessing of Heaven, and that which no man can
give we will give thee." Then they fetched the nine
bushels of flax-seed which Yspaddaden Penkawr
had required of Kilhwch, and they brought the full
measure, without lacking any, except one flax-seed,
and that the lame pismire brought in before night.

As Kai and Bedwyr sat on a beacon carn on the
summit of Plinlimmon, in the highest wind that ever
was in the world, they looked around them, and saw
a great smoke towards the south, afar off, which did
not bend with the wind. Then said Kai, "By the
hand of my friend, behold, yonder is the fire of a
robber!" Then they hastened towards the smoke,
and they came so near to it, that they could see Dillus
Varvawc scorching a wild Boar. "Behold, yonder is
the greatest robber that ever fled from Arthur," said
Bedwyr unto Kai. "Dost thou know him?" "I do
know him," answered Kai, "he is Dillus Varvawc,
and no leash in the world will be able to hold
Drudwyn, the cub of Greid the son of Eri, save a
leash made from the beard of him thou seest yonder.
And that even will be useless, unless his beard be
plucked alive with wooden tweezers; for if dead, it
will be brittle." "What thinkest thou that we should
do concerning this?" said Bedwyr. "Let us suffer
him," said Kai, "to eat as much as he will of the
meat, and after that he will fall asleep." And during
that time they employed themselves in making the
wooden tweezers. And when Kai knew certainly that
he was asleep, he made a pit under his feet, the largest

in the world, and he struck him a violent blow, and squeezed him into the pit. And there they twitched out his beard completely with the wooden tweezers ; and after that they slew him altogether.

And from thence they both went to Gelli Wic, in Cornwall, and took the leash made of Dillus Varvawc's beard with them, and they gave it unto Arthur's hand.

Then Arthur composed this Englyn,

> Kai made a leash
> Of Dillus son of Eurei's beard.
> Were he alive, thy death he'd be.

And thereupon Kai was wroth, so that the warriors of the Island could scarcely make peace between Kai and Arthur. And thenceforth, neither in Arthur's troubles, nor for the slaying of his men, would Kai come forward to his aid for ever after.

Said Arthur, "Which of the marvels is it best for us now to seek?" "It is best for us to seek Drudwyn, the cub of Greid, the son of Eri."

A little while before this, Creiddylad, the daughter of Lludd Llaw Ereint, and Gwythyr the son of Greidawl, were betrothed. And before she had become his bride, Gwyn ap Nudd came, and carried her away by force ; and Gwythyr the son of Greidawl gathered his host together, and went to fight with Gwyn ap Nudd. But Gwyn overcame him, and captured Greid the son of Eri, and Glinneu the son of Taran and Gwrgwst Ledlwm, and Dynvarth[1] his son. And he captured Penn the son of Nethawg, and Nwython, and Kyledyr Wyllt his son. And they slew Nwython, and took out his heart, and constrained Kyledyr to eat the heart of

---

[1] Dyvnarth.

his father. And therefrom Kyledyr became mad. When Arthur heard of this, he went to the North, and summoned Gwyn ap Nudd before him, and set free the nobles whom he had put in prison, and made peace between Gwyn ap Nudd and Gwythyr the son of Greidawl. And this was the peace that was made: that the maiden should remain in her father's house, without advantage to either of them, and that Gwyn ap Nudd and Gwythyr the son of Greidawl should fight for her every first of May, from thenceforth until the day of doom, and that whichever of them should then be conqueror should have the maiden.

And when Arthur had thus reconciled these chieftains, he obtained Mygdwn, Gweddw's horse, and the leash of Cwrs Cant Ewin.

And after that Arthur went into Armorica, and with him Mabon the son of Mellt, and Gware Gwallt Euryn, to seek the two dogs of Glythmyr Ledewic. And when he had got them, he went to the West of Ireland, in search of Gwrgi Severi; and Odgar the son of Aedd, king of Ireland, went with him. And thence went Arthur into the North, and captured Kyledyr Wyllt; and he went after Yskithyrwyn Penbaedd. And Mabon the son of Mellt came with the two dogs of Glythmyr Ledewic in his hand, and Drudwyn, the cub of Greid the son of Eri. And Arthur went himself to the chase, leading his own dog Cavall. And Kaw, of North Britain, mounted Arthur's mare Llamrei, and was first in the attack. Then Kaw, of North Britain, wielded a mighty axe, and absolutely daring he came valiantly up to the Boar, and clave his head in twain. And Kaw took away the tusk. Now the Boar was not slain by the dogs that Yspaddaden had mentioned, but by Cavall, Arthur's own dog.

And after Yskithyrwyn Penbaedd was killed, Arthur and his host departed to Gelli Wic in Cornwall. And thence he sent Menw the son of Teirgwaedd to see if the precious things were between the two ears of Twrch Trwyth, since it were useless to encounter him if they were not there. Albeit it was certain where he was, for he had laid waste the third part of Ireland. And Menw went to seek for him, and he met with him in Ireland, in Esgeir Oervel. And Menw took the form of a bird ; and he descended upon the top of his lair, and strove to snatch away one of the precious things from him, but he carried away nothing but one of his bristles. And the boar rose up angrily and shook himself so that some of his venom fell upon Menw, and he was never well from that day forward.

After this Arthur sent an embassy to Odgar, the son of Aedd, king of Ireland, to ask for the Cauldron of Diwrnach Wyddel, his purveyor. And Odgar commanded him to give it. But Diwrnach said, "Heaven is my witness, if it would avail him anything even to look at it, he should not do so." And the embassy of Arthur returned from Ireland with this denial. And Arthur set forward with a small retinue, and entered into Prydwen, his ship, and went over to Ireland. And they proceeded into the house of Diwrnach Wyddel. And the hosts of Odgar saw their strength. When they had eaten and drank as much as they desired, Arthur demanded to have the cauldron. And he answered, "If I would have given it to any one, I would have given it at the word of Odgar, king of Ireland."

When he had given them this denial, Bedwyr arose and seized hold of the cauldron, and placed it upon the back of Hygwyd, Arthur's servant, who was brother, by the mother's side, to Arthur's servant, Cachamwri. His office was always to carry Arthur's cauldron, and to place fire under it. And Llenlleawg Wyddel seized Caledvwlch, and brandished it. And they slew Diwrnach Wyddel and his company. Then came the Irish,[1] and fought with them. And when he had put them to flight, Arthur with his men went forward to the ship, carrying away the cauldron full of Irish money.[2] And he disembarked at the house of Llwydden[3] the son of Kelcoed, at Porth Kerddin in Dyved. And there is the measure of the cauldron.

Then Arthur summoned unto him all the warriors that were in the three Islands of Britain, and in the three Islands adjacent, and all that were in France and in Armorica, in Normandy and in the Summer Country, and all that were chosen footmen and valiant horsemen. And with all these, he went into Ireland. And in Ireland there was great fear and terror concerning him. And when Arthur had landed in the country, there came unto him the saints of Ireland and besought his protection. And he granted his protection unto them, and they gave him their blessing. Then the men of Ireland came unto Arthur, and brought him provisions. And Arthur went as far as Esgeir Oervel in Ireland, to the place where the Boar Trwyth was with his seven young pigs. And the dogs were let loose upon him from all sides. That day until evening, the Irish fought with him, nevertheless he laid waste the fifth part of Ireland. And on the day following the

[1] Hosts of Ireland.
[2] And when all the hosts had fled, Arthur and his men went to their ship in their sight, carrying with them the cauldron full of Irish money.
[3] Llwyddeu.

household of Arthur fought with him, and they were
worsted by him, and got no advantage. And the
third day Arthur himself encountered him, and he
fought with him nine nights and nine days without
so much as killing even one little pig.[1] The warriors
enquired of Arthur, what was the origin of that swine;
and he told them that he was once a king, and
that God had transformed him into a swine for his
sins.

Then Arthur sent Gwrhyr Gwalstawt Ieithoedd, to
endeavour to speak with him. And Gwrhyr assumed
the form of a bird, and alighted upon the top of the
lair, where he was with the seven young pigs. And
Gwrhyr Gwalstawt Icithoedd asked him, " By him who
turned you into this form, if you can speak, let some
one of you, I beseech you, come and talk with
Arthur." Grugyn Gwrych Ereint made answer to
him. (Now his bristles were like silver wire, and
whether he went through the wood or through the
plain, he was to be traced by the glittering of his
bristles.) And this was the answer that Grugyn
made, " By him who turned us into this form we
will not do so, and we will not speak with Arthur.
That we have been transformed thus is enough
for us to suffer, without your coming here to fight
with us." " I will tell you. Arthur comes but to
fight for the comb, and the razor, and the scissors,
which are between the two ears of Twrch Trwyth."
Said Grugyn, " Except he first take his life, he will
never have those precious things. And to-morrow
morning we will rise up hence, and we will go into
Arthur's country, and there will we do all the
mischief that we can."

[1] And he only killed one of his young pigs.

So they set forth through the sea towards Wales. And Arthur and his hosts, and his horses and his dogs, entered Prydwen, that they might encounter them without delay. Twrch Trwyth landed in Porth Cleis in Dyved, and the[1] came to Mynyw. The next day it was told to Arthur, that they had gone by, and he overtook them, as they were killing the cattle of Kynnwas Kwrr y Vagyl, having slain all that were at Aber Gleddyf, of man and beast, before the coming of Arthur.

Now when Arthur approached, Twrch Trwyth went on as far as Preseleu, and Arthur and his hosts followed him thither, and Arthur sent men to hunt him; Eli and Trachmyr, leading Drutwyn the whelp of Greid, the son of Eri, and Gwarthegyd the son of Kaw, in another quarter, with the two dogs of Glythmyr Ledewig, and Bedwyr leading Cavall, Arthur's own dog. And all the warriors ranged themselves around the Nyver. And there came there the three sons of Cleddyf Divwlch, men who had gained much fame at the slaying of Yskithyrwyn Penbaedd; and they went on from Glyn Nyver, and came to Cwm Kerwyn.

And there Twrch Trwyth made a stand, and slew four of Arthur's champions, Gwarthegyd the son of Kaw, and Tarawc of Allt Clwyd, and Rheidwn the son of Eli Atver, and Iscovan Hael. And after he had slain these men, he made a second stand in the same place. And there he slew Gwydre the son of Arthur, and Garselit Wyddel, and Glew the son of Ysgawd, and Iscawn the son of Panon; and there he himself was wounded.

And the next morning before it was day, some of

----

[1] Add "same night Arthur."

the men came up with him. And he slew Huandaw, and Gogigwr, and Penpingon, three attendants upon Glewlwyd Gavaelvawr, so that Heaven knows he had not an attendant remaining, excepting only Llaesgevyn, a man from whom no one ever derived any good. And together with these, he slew many of the men of that country, and Gwlydyn Saer, Arthur's chief Architect.

Then Arthur overtook him at Pelumyawc, and there he slew Madawc the son of Teithyon, and Gwyn the son of Tringad, the son of Neved, and Eiryawn Penllorau. Thence he went to Aberteivi,[1] where he made another stand, and where he slew Kyflas[2] the son of Kynan, and Gwilenhin king of France. Then he went as far as Glyn Ystu, and there the men and the dogs lost him.

Then Arthur summoned unto him Gwyn ab Nudd, and he asked him if he knew aught of Twrch Trwyth. And he said that he did not.

And all the huntsmen went to hunt the swine as far as Dyffryn Llychwr. And Grugyn Gwallt Ereint, and Llwydawg Govynnyad closed with them and killed all the huntsmen, so that there escaped but one man only. And Arthur and his hosts came to the place where Grugyn and Llwydawg were. And there he let loose the whole of the dogs upon them, and with the shout and barking that was set up, Twrch Trwyth came to their assistance.

And from the time that they came across the Irish sea, Arthur had never got sight of him until then.[3] So he set men and dogs upon him, and thereupon he started off and went to Mynydd Amanw.

---

[1] Aber Tywi.   [2] Kynlas.

[3] And ever since they had crossed the Irish Sea, he had not appeared to them until then.

And there one of his young pigs was killed.[1] Then they set upon him life for life, and Twrch Llawin was slain, and then there was slain another of the swine, Gwys was his name. After that he went on to Dyffryn Amanw, and there Banw and Bennwig were killed.[2] Of all his pigs there went with him alive from that place none save Grugyn Gwallt Ereint, and Llwydawg Govynnyad.

Thence he went on to Llwch Ewin, and Arthur overtook him there, and he made a stand. And there he slew Echel Forddwytwll, and Garwyli the son of Gwyddawg Gwyr, and many men and dogs likewise. And thence they went to Llwch Tawy. Grugyn Gwrych Ereint parted from them there, and went to Din Tywi. And thence he proceeded to Ceredigiawn, and Eli and Trachmyr with him, and a multitude likewise. Then he came to Garth Gregyn, and there Llwydawg Govynnyad fought in the midst of them, and slew Rhudvyw Rhys and many others with him. Then Llwydawg went thence to Ystrad Yw, and there the men of Armorica met him, and there he slew Hirpeissawg, the king of Armorica, and Llygatrudd Emys, and Gwrbothu, Arthur's uncles, his mother's brothers, and there was he himself slain.

Twrch Trwyth went from there to between Tawy and Euyas, and Arthur summoned all Cornwall and Devon unto him, to the estuary of the Severn, and he said to the warriors of this Island, "Twrch Trwyth has slain many of my men, but, by the valour of warriors, while I live he shall not go into Cornwall. And I will not follow him any longer, but I will oppose him life to life. Do ye as ye will." And he resolved that he would send a body of knights, with

[1] And there was killed a young boar from among his pigs.
[2] And there was killed a young boar and a young sow.

the dogs of the Island, as far as Euyas, who should
return thence to the Severn, and that tried warriors
should traverse the Island, and force him into the
Severn. And Mabon the son of Modron came up
with him at the Severn, upon Gwynn Mygddon, the
horse of Gweddw, and Goreu the son of Custennin,
and Menw the son of Teirgwaedd; this was betwixt
Llyn Lliwan and Aber Gwy. And Arthur fell upon
him together with the champions of Britain. And
Osla Kyllellvawr drew near, and Manawyddan the
son of Llyr, and Kacmwri the servant of Arthur, and
Gwyngelli, and they seized hold of him, catching him
first by his feet, and plunged him in the Severn,
so that it overwhelmed him. On the one side,
Mabon the son of Modron spurred his steed and
snatched his razor from him, and Kyledyr Wyllt came
up with him on the other side, upon another steed, in
the Severn, and took from him the scissors. But
before they could obtain the comb, he had regained
the ground with his feet, and from the moment that
he reached the shore, neither dog, nor man, nor
horse could overtake him until he came to Cornwall.
If they had had trouble in getting the jewels from
him, much more had they in seeking to save the two
men from being drowned. Kacmwri, as they drew
him forth, was dragged by two millstones into the
deep. And as Osla Kyllellvawr was running after
the Boar his knife had dropped out of the sheath, and
he had lost it, and after that the sheath became full
of water, and its weight drew him down into the
deep, as they were drawing him forth.

Then Arthur and his hosts proceeded until they
overtook the Boar in Cornwall, and the trouble which
they had met with before was mere play to what
they encountered in seeking the comb. But from one

difficulty to another, the comb was at length obtained.
And then he was hunted from Cornwall, and driven
straight forward into the deep sea.   And thenceforth
it was never known whither he went; and Aned and
Aethlem with him.   Then went Arthur to Gelliwic,
in Cornwall, to anoint himself, and to rest from his
fatigues.

Said Arthur, "Is there any one of the marvels yet
unobtained?"   Said one of his men, "There is—the
blood of the witch Orddu, the daughter of the witch
Orwen, of Penn Nant Govid, on the confines of
Hell."   Arthur set forth towards the North, and
came to the place where was the witch's cave.   And
Gwyn ab Nudd, and Gwythyr the son of Greidawl,
counselled him to send Kacmwri, and Hygwyd his
brother to fight with the witch.   And as they entered
the cave, the witch seized upon them, and she caught
Hygwyd by the hair of his head, and threw him on
the floor beneath her.   And Kacmwri caught her by the
hair of her head, and dragged her to the earth from
off Hygwyd, but she turned again upon them both,[1]
and drove them both out with kicks and with cuffs.
And Arthur was wroth at seeing his two attendants
almost slain, and he sought to enter the cave ; but
Gwyn and Gwythyr said unto him, "It would not be
fitting or seemly for us to see thee squabbling with a
hag.   Let Hiramren, and Hireidil go to the cave."
So they went.   But if great was the trouble of the
two first that went, much greater was that of these
two.   And Heaven knows that not one of the four
could move from the spot, until they placed them all
upon Llamrei, Arthur's mare.   And then Arthur rushed
to the door of the cave, and at the door, he struck at

[1] But she turned again upon Kacmwri ; she beat both men
soundly, disarmed them, and drove them out.

the witch, with Carnwennan his dagger, and clove her
in twain, so that she fell in two parts. And Kaw, of
North Britain, took the blood of the witch and kept it.

Then Kilhwch set forward, and Goreu, the son of
Custennin, with him, and as many as wished ill
to Yspaddaden Penkawr. And they took the marvels
with them to his Court. And Kaw of North Britain
came and shaved his beard, skin and flesh, clean off
to the very bone from ear to ear. " Art thou shaved,
man?" said Kilhwch. " I am shaved," answered he.
"Is thy daughter mine now?" "She is thine," said
he, " but therefore needest thou not thank me, but
Arthur who hath accomplished this for thee. By my
free will thou shouldest never have had her, for with
her I lose my life." Then Goreu the son of Custennin, seized him by the hair of his head, and dragged
him after him to the keep, and cut off his head, and
placed it on a stake on the citadel. Then they took
possession of his castle, and of his treasures.

And that night Olwen became Kilhwch's bride,
and she continued to be his wife as long as she
lived. And the hosts of Arthur dispersed themselves,
each man to his own country. And thus did Kilhwch
obtain Olwen the daughter of Yspaddaden Penkawr.

60

PEREDUR THE SON OF EVRAWC.

EARL EVRAWC owned the Earldom of the North. And he had seven sons. And Evrawc maintained himself not so much by his own possessions as by attending tournaments, and wars, and combats. And, as it often befalls those who join in encounters and wars, he was slain, and six of his sons likewise. Now the name of his seventh son was Peredur, and he was the youngest of them. And he was not of an age to go

to wars and encounters, otherwise he might have been
slain as his father and brothers. His mother was a
scheming and thoughtful woman, and she was very
solicitous concerning this her only son and his [1] possessions. So she took counsel with herself to leave
the inhabited country, and to flee to the deserts and
unfrequented wildernesses. And she permitted none
to bear her company thither but women and boys,
and spiritless men, who were both unaccustomed and
unequal to war and fighting. And none dared to
bring either horses or arms where her son was, lest
he should set his mind upon them. And the youth
went daily to divert himself in the forest, by flinging
sticks and staves. And one day he saw his mother's
flock of goats, and near the goats two hinds were
standing. And he marvelled greatly that these two
should be without horns, while the others had them.
And he thought they had long run wild and on
that account they had lost their horns. And by
activity and swiftness of foot, he drove the hinds and
the goats together into the house which there was
for the goats at the extremity of the forest. Then
Peredur returned to his mother. "Ah, mother,"
said he, "a marvellous thing have I seen in the
wood; two of thy goats have run wild, and lost
their horns; through their having been so long
missing in the wood. And no man had ever more
trouble than I had to drive them in." Then they
all arose and went to see. And when they beheld
the hinds, they were greatly astonished.

And one day they saw three knights coming along
the horse-road on the borders of the forest. And
the three knights were Gwalchmai the son of Gwyar,
and Geneir Gwystyl, and Owain the son of Urien

[1] Her.

And Owain kept on the track of the knight who had divided the apples in Arthur's Court, whom they were in pursuit of. "Mother," said Peredur, "what are those yonder?" "They are angels, my son," said she. "By my faith," said Peredur, "I will go and become an angel with them." And Peredur went to the road, and met them. "Tell me, good soul," said Owain, "sawest thou a knight pass this way, either to-day or yesterday?" "I know not," answered he, "what a knight is." "Such an one as I am," said Owain. "If thou wilt tell me what I ask thee, I will tell thee that which thou askest me." "Gladly will I do so," replied Owain. "What is this?" demanded Peredur, concerning the saddle. "It is a saddle," said Owain. Then he asked about all the accoutrements which he saw upon the men, and the horses, and the arms, and what they were for, and how they were used. And Owain shewed him all these things fully, and told him what use was made of them. "Go forward," said Peredur, "for I saw such an one as thou enquirest for, and I will follow thee."

Then Peredur returned to his mother and her company, and he said to her, "Mother, those were not angels, but honourable knights." Then his mother swooned away. And Peredur went to the place where they kept the horses that carried firewood, and that brought meat and drink from the inhabited country to the desert. And he took a bony piebald horse, which seemed to him the strongest of them. And he pressed a pack into the form of a saddle, and with twisted twigs he imitated the trappings which he had seen upon the horses. And when Peredur came again to his mother, the Countess had recovered from her swoon. "My son," said she,

"desirest thou to ride forth?" "Yes, with thy
leave," said he. "Wait then, that I may counsel
thee before thou goest." "Willingly," he answered,
"speak quickly." "Go forward," then she said, "to
the Court of Arthur, where there are the best, and
the boldest, and the most bountiful of men. And
wherever thou seest a church, repeat there thy Paternoster unto it. And if thou see meat and drink,
and hast need of them, and none have the kindness
or the courtesy to give them to thee, take them
thyself. If thou hear an outcry, proceed towards it,
especially if it be the outcry of a woman. If thou
see a fair jewel, possess thyself of it, and give it to
another, for thus thou shalt obtain praise. If thou
see a fair woman, pay thy court to her, whether
she will or no; for thus thou wilt render thyself a
better and more esteemed man than thou wast
before."

After this discourse, Peredur mounted the horse,
and taking a handful of sharp pointed forks in his
hand, he rode forth. And he journeyed two days
and two nights in the woody wildernesses, and in
desert places, without food and without drink. And
then he came to a vast wild wood, and far within
the wood he saw a fair even glade, and in the
glade he saw a tent, and seeming to him to be a
church, he repeated his Paternoster to the tent. And
he went towards it, and the door of the tent was
open. And a golden chair was near the door. And
on the chair sat a lovely auburn-haired maiden, with
a golden frontlet on her forehead, and sparkling
stones in the frontlet, and with a large gold ring on
her hand. And Peredur dismounted, and entered
the tent. And the maiden was glad at his coming,
and bade him welcome. At the entrance of the

tent he saw food, and two flasks full of wine, and two
loaves of fine wheaten flour, and collops of the flesh
of the wild boar. "My mother told me," said Peredur,
"wheresoever I saw meat and drink, to take it."
"Take the meat and welcome, chieftain," said she.
So Peredur took half of the meat and of the liquor
himself, and left the rest to the maiden. And when
Peredur had finished eating, he bent upon his knee
before the maiden. "My mother," said he, "told
me, wheresoever I saw a fair jewel, to take it." "Do
so, my soul," said she. So Peredur took the ring.
And he mounted his horse, and proceeded on his
journey.

After this, behold the knight came, to whom the
tent belonged; and he was the Lord of the Glade.
And he saw the track of the horse, and he said to
the maiden, "Tell me who has been here since I
departed." "A man," said she, "of wonderful
demeanour." And she described to him what
Peredur's appearance and conduct had been. "Tell
me," said he, "did he offer thee any wrong?"
"No," answered the maiden, "by my faith, he
harmed me not." "By my faith, I do not believe
thee; and until I can meet with him, and revenge
the insult he has done me, and wreak my vengeance
upon him, thou shalt not remain two nights in the
same house." And the knight arose, and set forth to
seek Peredur.

Meanwhile Peredur journeyed on towards Arthur's
Court. And before he reached it, another knight
had been there, who gave a ring of thick gold at the
door of the gate for holding his horse, and went
into the Hall where Arthur and his household, and
Gwenhwyvar and her maidens, were assembled. And
the page of the chamber was serving Gwenhwyvar

with a golden goblet. Then the knight dashed the
liquor that was therein upon her face, and upon her
stomacher, and gave her a violent blow on the face,
and said, "If any have the boldness to dispute this
goblet with me, and to avenge the insult to Gwenhwyvar, let him follow me to the meadow, and there
I will await him." So the knight took his horse, and
rode to the meadow. And all the household hung
down their heads, lest any of them should be re-
quested to go and avenge the insult to Gwenhwyvar.
For it seemed to them, that no one would have
ventured on so daring an outrage, unless he possessed
such powers, through magic or charms, that none
could be able to take vengeance upon him. Then,
behold Peredur entered the Hall, upon the bony
piebald horse, with the uncouth trappings upon it;
and in this way he traversed the whole length of
the Hall.[1] In the centre of the Hall stood Kai.
"Tell me, tall man," said Peredur, "is that Arthur,
yonder?" "What wouldest thou with Arthur?"
asked Kai. "My mother told me to go to Arthur,
and receive the honour of knighthood." "By my
faith," said he, "thou art all too meanly equipped
with horse and with arms." Thereupon he was perceived by all the household, and they threw sticks
at him. Then, behold, a dwarf came forward. He
had already been a year at Arthur's Court, both he
and a female dwarf. They had craved harbourage of
Arthur, and had obtained it; and during the whole
year, neither of them had spoken a single word to
any one. When the dwarf beheld Peredur, "Ha ha!"
said he, "the welcome of Heaven be unto thee,
goodly Peredur, son of Evrawc, the chief of warriors,
and flower of knighthood." "Truly," said Kai, "thou

[1] And very unmeet for so honourable a Court.

art ill-taught to remain a year mute at Arthur's Court,
with choice of society; and now, before the face of
Arthur and all his household, to call out, and declare
such a man as this the chief of warriors, and the
flower of knighthood." And he gave him such a
box on the ear, that he fell senseless to the ground.
Then exclaimed the female dwarf, " Ha ha! goodly
Peredur, son of Evrawc; the welcome of Heaven be
unto thee, flower of knights, and light of chivalry."
"Of a truth, maiden," said Kai, "thou art ill-bred to
remain mute for a year at the Court of Arthur and
then to speak as thou dost of such a man as this."
And Kai kicked her with his foot, so that she fell to
the ground senseless. "Tall man," said Peredur,
"show me which is Arthur." "Hold thy peace,"
said Kai, "and go after the knight who went hence
to the meadow, and take from him the goblet, and overthrow him, and possess thyself of his horse and arms,
and then thou shalt receive the order of knighthood."
"I will do so, tall man," said Peredur. So he turned
his horse's head towards the meadow. And when he
came there, the knight was riding up and down,
proud of his strength, and valour, and noble mien.
" Tell me," said the knight, "didst thou see any one
coming after me from the Court?" "The tall man
that was there," said he, "desired me to come, and
overthrow thee, and to take from thee the goblet,
and thy horse and thy armour for myself." "Silence,"
said the knight; "go back to the Court, and tell
Arthur, from me, either to come himself, or to send
some other to fight with me ; and unless he do so
quickly, I will not wait for him." " By my faith,"
said Peredur, "choose thou whether it shall be
willingly or unwillingly, but I will have the horse,
and the arms, and the goblet." And upon this the

knight ran at him furiously, and struck him a violent
blow[1] with the shaft of his spear, between the neck
and the shoulder. "Ha ha! lad," said Peredur, "my
mother's servants were not used to play with me in
this wise; therefore, thus will I play with thee."
And thereupon he struck him with a sharp pointed
fork, and it hit him in the eye, and came out at the
back of his neck, so that he instantly fell down lifeless.

"Verily," said Owain the son of Urien to Kai,
"thou wert ill advised, when thou didst send that
madman after the knight. For one of two things
must befall him. He must either be overthrown, or
slain. If he is overthrown by the knight, he will be
counted by him to be an honourable person of the
Court, and an eternal disgrace will it be to Arthur
and his warriors. And if he is slain, the disgrace
will be the same, and moreover, his sin will be upon
him; therefore will I go to see what has befallen
him." So Owain went to the meadow, and he found
Peredur dragging the man about. "What art thou

[1] Add "causing a grievous wound."

doing thus?" said Owain. "This iron coat," said
Peredur, "will never come from off him; not by my
efforts, at any rate."[1] And Owain unfastened his
armour and his clothes. "Here, my good soul,"
said he, "is a horse and armour better than thine.
Take them joyfully, and come with me to Arthur,
to receive the order of knighthood, for thou dost
merit it." "May I never shew my face again, if I
go," said Peredur, "but take thou the goblet to
Gwenhwyvar, and tell Arthur, that wherever I am,
I will be his vassal, and will do him what profit and
service I am able. And say that I will not come
to his Court, until I have encountered the tall man
that is there, to avenge the injury he did to the
dwarf and dwarfess." And Owain went back to the
Court, and related all these things to Arthur and
Gwenhwyvar, and to all the household.[2]

And Peredur rode forward. And as he proceeded,
behold a knight met him. "Whence comest thou?"
said the knight. "I come from Arthur's Court," said
Peredur. "Art thou one of his men?" asked he.
"Yes, by my faith," he answered. "A good service,
truly, is that of Arthur." "Wherefore sayest thou
so?" said Peredur. "I will tell thee," said he, "I
have always been Arthur's enemy, and all such of his
men as I have ever encountered, I have slain." And
without further parlance, they fought, and it was not
long before Peredur brought him to the ground, over
his horse's crupper. Then the knight besought his
mercy. "Mercy thou shalt have," said Peredur, "if
thou wilt make oath to me, that thou wilt go to
Arthur's Court, and tell him that it was I that over-

---

[1] "This iron coat will never come off him," said Peredur.
"I doubt whether it is not part of himself, born with him."
[2] Add "and the threat against Kai."

threw thee, for the honour of his service; and say
that I will never come to the Court, until I have
avenged the insult offered to the dwarf and dwarfess."
The knight pledged him his faith of this, and proceeded to the Court of Arthur, and said as he had
promised, and conveyed the threat to Kai.

And Peredur rode forward. And within that week
he encountered sixteen knights, and overthrew them
all shamefully. And they all went to Arthur's Court,
taking with them the same message which the first
knight had conveyed from Peredur, and the same
threat which he had sent to Kai. And thereupon
Kai was reproved by Arthur; and Kai was greatly
grieved thereat.

And Peredur rode forward. And he came to a
vast and desert wood, on the confines of which was
a lake. And on the other side was a fair castle.
And on the border of the lake he saw a venerable
hoary-headed man sitting upon a velvet cushion, and
having a garment of velvet upon him. And his attendants were fishing in the lake. When the hoary-
headed man beheld Peredur approaching, he arose,
and went towards the castle. And the old man was
lame. Peredur rode to the palace, and the door was
open, and he entered the hall. And there was the
hoary-headed man sitting on a cushion, and a large
blazing fire burning before him. And the household
and the company arose to meet Peredur, and disarrayed him. And the man asked the youth to sit
on the cushion; and they sat down, and conversed
together. When it was time, the tables were laid,
and they went to meat. And when they had finished
their meal, the man enquired of Peredur, if he knew
well how to fight with the sword. "I know not,"
said Peredur, " but were I to be taught, doubtless I

should." "Whoever can play well with the cudgel
and shield, will also be able to fight with a sword."
And the man had two sons; the one had yellow hair,
and the other auburn. "Arise, youth," said he,
"and play with the cudgel and the shield." And
so did they. "Tell me, my soul," said the man,
"which of the youths thinkest thou plays best?" "I
think," said Peredur, "that the yellow-haired youth
could draw blood from the other, if he chose."
"Arise thou, my life, and take the cudgel and the
shield from the hand of the youth with the auburn
hair, and draw blood from the yellow-haired youth,
if thou canst." So Peredur arose, and went to play
with the yellow-haired youth; and he lifted up his
arm, and struck him such a mighty blow, that his
brow fell over his eye, and the blood flowed forth.
"Ah, my life," said the man, "come now, and sit
down, for thou wilt become the best fighter with the
sword of any in this island; and I am thy uncle, thy
mother's brother. And with me shalt thou remain
a space, in order to learn the manners and customs
of different countries, and courtesy, and gentleness,
and noble bearing. Leave, then, the habits and the
discourse of thy mother, and I will be thy teacher;
and I will raise thee to the rank of knight from this
time forward. And thus do thou. If thou seest
aught to cause thee wonder, ask not the meaning of
it; if no one has the courtesy to inform thee, the
reproach will not fall upon thee, but upon me that
am thy teacher." And they had abundance of honour
and service. And when it was time, they went to
sleep. At the break of day, Peredur arose, and took
his horse, and with his uncle's permission, he rode
forth. And he came to a vast desert wood, and at
the further end of the wood was a meadow, and on

the other side of the meadow he saw a large castle.
And thitherward Peredur bent his way, and he found
the gate open, and he proceeded to the hall. And
he beheld a stately hoary-headed man sitting on one
side of the hall, and many pages around him, who
arose to receive and to honour Peredur. And they
placed him by the side of the owner of the palace.
Then they discoursed together; and when it was
time to eat, they caused Peredur to sit beside the
nobleman during the repast. And when they had
eaten and drank as much as they desired, the nobleman asked Peredur, whether he could fight with a
sword? "Were I to receive instruction," said
Peredur, "I think I could." Now, there was on
the floor of the hall a huge staple, as large as a
warrior could grasp. "Take yonder sword," said
the man to Peredur, "and strike the iron staple."
So Peredur arose, and struck the staple, so that he
cut it in two; and the sword broke into two parts
also. "Place the two parts together, and reunite
them," and Peredur placed them together, and they
became entire as they were before. And a second
time he struck upon the staple, so that both it and
the sword broke in two, and as before they reunited.
And the third time he gave a like blow, and placed
the broken parts together, and neither the staple nor
the sword would unite, as before. "Youth," said the
nobleman, "come now, and sit down, and my blessing be upon thee. Thou fightest best with the sword
of any man in the kingdom. Thou hast arrived at
two-thirds of thy strength, and the other third thou
hast not yet obtained; and when thou attainest to
thy full power, none will be able to contend with
thee. I am thy uncle, thy mother's brother, and I
am brother [1] to the man in whose house thou wast

---

[1] We are brother and sister.

last night." Then Peredur and his uncle discoursed together, and he beheld two youths enter the hall, and proceed up to the chamber, bearing a spear of mighty size, with three streams of blood flowing from

the point to the ground. And when all the company saw this, they began wailing and lamenting. But for all that, the man did not break off his discourse with Peredur. And as he did not tell Peredur the meaning of what he saw, he forebore to ask him concerning it. And when the clamour had a little subsided, behold two maidens entered, with a large salver between them, in which was .a man's head, surrounded by a profusion of blood. And thereupon the company of the court made so great an outcry, that it was irksome to be in the same hall with them. But at length they were silent. And when time was that they should sleep, Peredur was brought into a fair chamber.

And the next day, with his uncle's permission, he rode forth. And he came to a wood, and far within the wood he heard a loud cry, and he saw a beautiful woman with auburn hair, and a horse with a saddle upon it, standing near her, and a corpse by her side. And as she strove to place the corpse upon the horse, it fell to the ground, and thereupon she made a great lamentation. "Tell me, sister," said Peredur, "wherefore art thou bewailing?" "Oh! accursed Peredur, little pity has my ill fortune ever met with from thee." "Wherefore," said Peredur, "am I accursed?" "Because thou wast the cause of thy mother's death; for when thou didst ride forth against her will, anguish seized upon her heart, so that she died; and therefore art thou accursed. And the dwarf and the dwarfess that thou sawest at Arthur's Court, were the dwarfs of thy father and mother; and I am thy foster-sister, and this was my wedded husband, and he was slain by the knight that is in the glade in the wood; and do not thou go near him, lest thou shouldest be slain by him likewise." "My sister, thou dost reproach me wrongfully; through my having so long remained amongst you, I shall scarcely vanquish him; and had I continued longer it would, indeed, be difficult for me to succeed. Cease, therefore, thy lamenting, for it is of no avail,

and I will bury the body, and then I will go in quest
of the knight, and see if I can do vengeance upon
him." And when he had buried the body, they went
to the place where the knight was, and found him
riding proudly along the glade; and he enquired
of Peredur whence he came. "I come from Arthur's
Court." "And art thou one of Arthur's men?"
"Yes, by my faith." "A profitable alliance, truly,
is that of Arthur." And without further parlance,
they encountered one another, and immediately
Peredur overthrew the knight, and he besought
mercy of Peredur. "Mercy shalt thou have," said
he, "upon these terms, that thou take this woman
in marriage, and do her all the honour and reverence
in thy power, seeing thou hast, without cause, slain
her wedded husband; and that thou go to Arthur's
Court, and shew him that it was I that overthrew
thee, to do him honour and service; and that thou
tell him that I will never come to his Court again
until I have met with the tall man that is there, to
take vengeance upon him for his insult to the dwarf
and the dwarfess." And he took the knight's as-
surance, that he would perform all this. Then the
knight provided the lady with a horse and garments
that were suitable for her, and took her with him to
Arthur's Court. And he told Arthur all that had
occurred, and gave the defiance to Kai. And Arthur
and all his household reproved Kai, for having driven
such a youth as Peredur from his Court.

Said Owain the son of Urien, "This youth will
never come into the Court until Kai has gone forth
from it." "By my faith," said Arthur, "I will search
all the deserts in the island of Britain, until I find
Peredur, and then let him and his adversary do their
utmost to each other."

E

Then Peredur rode forward. And he came to a desert wood, where he saw not the track either of men or animals, and where there was nothing but bushes and weeds. And at the upper end of the wood he saw a vast castle, wherein were many strong towers ; and when he came near .the gate, he found the weeds taller than he had done elsewhere. And he struck the gate with the shaft of his lance, and thereupon behold a lean auburn-haired youth came to an opening in the battlements. " Choose thou, chieftain," said he. " Whether shall I open the gate unto thee, or shall I announce unto those that are chief, that thou art at the gateway ? " " Say that I am here," said Peredur, " and if it is desired that I should enter, I will go in." And the youth came back, and opened the gate for Peredur. And when he went into the hall, he beheld eighteen youths, lean and red-headed, of the same height and of the same aspect, and of the same dress, and of the same age as the one who had opened the gate for him. And they were well skilled in courtesy and in service. And they disarrayed him. Then they sat down to discourse. Thereupon, behold five maidens came from the chamber into the hall. And Peredur was certain that he had never seen another of so fair an aspect as the chief of the maidens. And she had an old garment of satin upon her, which had once been handsome, but was then so tattered, that her skin could be seen through it. And whiter was her skin than the bloom of crystal, and her hair and her two eyebrows were blacker than jet, and on her cheeks were two red spots, redder than whatever is reddest. And the maiden welcomed Peredur, and put her arms about his neck, and made him sit down beside her. Not long after this he saw two nuns enter and a

flask full of wine was borne by one, and six loaves
of white bread by the other. "Lady," said they,
"Heaven is witness, that there is not so much of
food and liquor as this left in yonder Convent this
night." Then they went to meat, and Peredur
observed that the maiden wished to give more of
the food and of the liquor to him than to any of
the others. "My sister," said Peredur, "I will share
out the food and the liquor." "Not so, my soul,"
said she. "By my faith, but I will." So Peredur
took the bread, and he gave an equal portion of it
to each alike, as well as a cup full of the liquor.
And when it was time for them to sleep, a chamber
was prepared for Peredur, and he went to rest.

"Behold, sister," said the youths to the fairest and
most exalted of the maidens, "we have counsel for
thee." "What may it be?" she enquired. "Go to
the youth that is in the upper chamber, and offer to
become his wife, or the lady of his love, if it seem
well to him." "That were indeed unfitting," said
she. "Hitherto I have not been the lady love of
any knight, and to make him such an offer before I
am wooed by him, that, truly, can I not do." "By
our confession to Heaven, unless thou actest thus,
we will leave thee here to thy enemies, to do as they
will with thee." And through fear of this, the maiden
went forth; and shedding tears, she proceeded to the
chamber. And with the noise of the door opening,
Peredur awoke; and the maiden was weeping and
lamenting. "Tell me, my sister," said Peredur,
"wherefore dost thou weep?" "I will tell thee,
lord," said she, "my father possessed these dominions
as their chief, and this palace was his, and with it
he held the best earldom in the kingdom; then the
son of another earl sought me of my father, and I

was not willing to be given unto him, and my father would not give me against my will, either to him or any earl in the world. And my father had no child except myself. And after my father's death, these dominions came into my own hands, and then was I less willing to accept him than before. So he made war upon me, and conquered all my possessions except this one house. And through the valour of the men whom thou hast seen, who are my foster brothers, and the strength of the house, it can never be taken while food and drink remain. And now our provisions are exhausted; but as thou hast seen, we have been fed by the nuns, to whom the country is free. And at length they also are without supply of food or liquor. And at no later date than to-morrow, the earl will come against this place with all his forces; and if I fall into his power, my fate will be no better than to be given over to the grooms of his horses. Therefore, lord, I am come to offer to place myself in thy hands, that thou mayest succour me, either by taking me hence, or by defending me here, whichever may seem best unto thee." "Go, my sister," said he, "and sleep; nor will I depart from thee until I do that which thou requirest, or prove whether I can assist thee or not." The maiden went again to rest; and the next morning she came to Peredur, and saluted him. "Heaven prosper thee, my soul, and what tidings dost thou bring?" "None other, than that the earl and all his forces have alighted at the gate, and I never beheld any place so covered with tents, and thronged with knights challenging others to the combat." "Truly," said Peredur, "let my horse be made ready." So his horse was accoutred, and he arose, and sallied forth to the meadow. And there was a knight riding proudly along the meadow, having raised the signal for battle. And they encountered, and Peredur threw the knight over his horse's crupper to the ground. And at the close of the day, one of the chief knights came to fight with him, and he overthrew him also, so that he besought his mercy. " Who art thou ? " said Peredur. " Verily," said he, " I am Master of the Household to the earl." " And how much of the Countess's possessions is there in thy power ? " " The third part, verily," answered he. " Then," said Peredur, " restore to her the third of her possessions in full, and all the profit thou hast made by them, and bring meat and drink for a hundred men, with their horses and arms, to her court this night. And thou shalt remain her captive, unless she wish to take thy life." And this he did forthwith. And that night the maiden was right joyful, and they fared plenteously.

And the next day Peredur rode forth to the meadow ; and that day he vanquished a multitude of the host. And at the close of the day, there came a proud and stately knight, and Peredur overthrew him, and he besought his mercy. " Who art thou ? " said Peredur. " I am Steward of the Palace," said he. " And how much of the maiden's possessions are under thy control ? " " One third part," answered he. " Verily," said Peredur, " thou shalt fully restore to the maiden her possessions, and, moreover, thou shalt give her meat and drink for two hundred men, and their horses and their arms. And for thyself, thou shalt be her captive." And immediately it was so done.

And the third day Peredur rode forth to the meadow ; and he vanquished more that day than on either of the preceding. And at the close of the

day, an earl came to encounter him, and he overthrew him, and he besought his mercy. "Who art
thou?" said Peredur. "I am the earl," said he.
"I will not conceal it from thee." "Verily," said
Peredur, "thou shalt restore the whole of the
maiden's earldom, and shalt give her thine own
earldom in addition thereto, and meat and drink
for three hundred men, and their horses and arms,
and thou thyself shalt remain in her power." And
thus it was fulfilled. And Peredur tarried three
weeks in the country, causing tribute and obedience
to be paid to the maiden, and the government to
be placed in her hands. "With thy leave," said
Peredur, "I will go hence." "Verily, my brother,
desirest thou this?" "Yes, by my faith; and had
it not been for love of thee, I should not have been
here thus long." "My soul," said she, "who art
thou?" "I am Peredur the son of Evrawc from
the North; and if ever thou art in trouble or in
danger, acquaint me therewith, and if I can, I will
protect thee."

So Peredur rode forth. And far thence there met
him a lady, mounted on a horse that was lean, and
covered with sweat; and she saluted the youth.
"Whence comest thou, my sister?" Then she told
him the cause of her journey. Now she was the
wife of the Lord of the Glade. "Behold," said he,
"I am the knight through whom thou art in trouble,
and he shall repent it, who has treated thee thus."
Thereupon, behold a knight rode up, and he enquired
of Peredur, if he had seen a knight such as he was
seeking. "Hold thy peace," said Peredur, "I am
he whom thou seekest; and by my faith, thou
deservest ill of thy household for thy treatment of
the maiden, for she is innocent concerning me." So

they encountered, and they were not long in combat
ere Peredur overthrew the knight, and he besought
his mercy. "Mercy thou shalt have," said Peredur,
"so thou wilt return by the way thou camest, and
declare that thou holdest the maiden innocent, and
so that thou wilt acknowledge unto her the reverse
thou hast sustained at my hands." And the knight
plighted him his faith thereto.

Then Peredur rode forward. And above him he
beheld a castle, and thitherward he went. And he
struck upon the gate with his lance, and then, behold
a comely auburn-haired youth opened the gate, and
he had the stature of a warrior, and the years of a
boy. And when Peredur came into the hall, there
was a tall and stately lady sitting in a chair, and
many handmaidens around her; and the lady rejoiced at his coming. And when it was time, they
went to meat. And after their repast was finished,
"It were well for thee, chieftain," said she, "to go
elsewhere to sleep." "Wherefore can I not sleep
here?" said Peredur. "Nine sorceresses are here,
my soul, of the sorceresses of Gloucester, and their
father and their mother are with them; and unless
we can make our escape before daybreak, we shall
be slain; and already they have conquered and laid
waste all the country, except this one dwelling."
"Behold," said Peredur, "I will remain here to-night,
and if you are in trouble, I will do you what service
I can; but harm shall you not receive from me." So
they went to rest. And with the break of day,
Peredur heard a dreadful outcry. And he hastily
arose, and went forth in his vest and his doublet,
with his sword about his neck, and he saw a sorceress
overtake one of the watch, who cried out violently.
Peredur attacked the sorceress, and struck her upon

the head with his sword, so that he flattened her helmet and her headpiece like a dish upon her head. "Thy mercy, goodly Peredur, son of Evrawc, and the mercy of Heaven." "How knowest thou, hag, that I am Peredur?" "By destiny, and the fore-knowledge that I should suffer harm from thee. And thou shalt take a horse and armour of me; and with me thou shalt go to learn chivalry and the use of thy arms." Said Peredur, "Thou shalt have mercy, if thou pledge thy faith thou wilt never more injure the dominions of the Countess." And Peredur took surety of this, and with permission of the Countess, he set forth with the sorceress to the palace of the sorceresses. And there he remained for three weeks, and then he made choice of a horse and arms, and went his way.

And in the evening he entered a valley, and at the head of the valley he came to a hermit's cell, and the hermit welcomed him gladly, and there he spent the night. And in the morning he arose, and when he went forth, behold a shower of snow had fallen the night before, and a hawk had killed a wild fowl in front of the cell. And the noise of the horse scared the hawk away, and a raven alighted upon the bird. And Peredur stood, and compared the blackness of the raven, and whiteness of the snow, and the redness of the blood, to the hair of the lady that best he loved, which was blacker than jet, and to her skin which was whiter than the snow, and to the two red spots upon her cheeks, which were redder than the blood upon the snow appeared to be.

Now Arthur and his household were in search of Peredur. "Know ye," said Arthur, "who is the knight with the long spear that stands by the brook[1]

[1] In the dingle.

up yonder?" "Lord," said one of them, "I will
go and learn who he is." So the youth came to the
place where Peredur was, and asked him what he
did thus, and who he was. And from the intensity
with which he thought upon the lady whom best
he loved, he gave him no answer. Then the youth
thrust at Peredur with his lance, and Peredur turned
upon him, and struck him over his horse's crupper
to the ground. And after this, four and twenty
youths came to him, and he did not answer one
more than another, but gave the same reception to
all, bringing them with one single thrust to the
ground. And then came Kai, and spoke to Peredur
rudely and angrily; and Peredur took him with his
lance under the jaw, and cast him from him with a
thrust, so that he broke his arm and his shoulder
blade, and he rode over him one and twenty times.
And while he lay thus, stunned with the violence of
the pain that he had suffered, his horse returned
back at a wild and prancing pace. And when the
household saw the horse come back without his
rider, they rode forth in haste to the place where
the encounter had been. And when they first came
there, they thought that Kai was slain; but they
found that if he had a skilful physician, he yet
might live. And Peredur moved not from his meditation, on seeing the concourse that was around Kai.
And Kai was brought to Arthur's tent, and Arthur
caused skilful physicians to come to him. And
Arthur was grieved that Kai had met with this reverse, for he loved him greatly.

"Then," said Gwalchmai, "it is not fitting that any
should disturb an honourable knight from his thought
unadvisedly ; for either he is pondering some damage
that he has sustained, or he is thinking of the lady

whom best he loves.   And through such ill-advised
proceeding, perchance this misadventure has befallen
him who last met with him.   And if it seem well
to thee, lord, I will go and see if this knight has
changed from his thought; and if he has, I will
ask him courteously to come and visit thee."   Then
Kai was wrath, and he spoke angry and spiteful
words.   "Gwalchmai," said he, "I know that thou
wilt bring him because he is fatigued.   Little praise
and honour, nevertheless, wilt thou have from van-
quishing a weary knight, who is tired with fighting.
Yet, thus hast thou gained the advantage over many.
And while thy speech and thy soft words last, a coat
of thin linen were armour sufficient for thee, and thou
wilt not need to break either lance or sword in fighting with the knight in the state he is in."   Then
said Gwalchmai to Kai, "Thou mightest use more
pleasant words, wert thou so minded ; and it behoves
thee not upon me to wreak thy wrath and thy dis-
pleasure.   Methinks I shall bring the knight hither
with me without breaking either my arm or my
shoulder."   Then said Arthur to Gwalchmai, "Thou
speakest like a wise and a prudent man; go and
take enough of armour about thee, and choose thy
horse."   And Gwalchmai accoutred himself, and rode
forward hastily to the place where Peredur was.

And Peredur was resting on the shaft of his spear,
pondering the same thought, and Gwalchmai came
to him without any signs of hostility, and said to him,
"If I thought that it would be as agreeable to thee as
it would be to me, I would converse with thee.   I
have also a message from Arthur unto thee, to pray
thee to come and visit him.   And two men have
been before on this errand."   "That is true," said
Peredur, "and uncourteously they came.   They at-

tacked me, and I was annoyed thereat, for it was not
pleasing to me to be drawn from the thought that I
was in, for I was thinking of the lady whom best I
love; and thus was she brought to my mind,—I was
looking upon the snow, and upon the raven, and
upon the drops of the blood of the bird that the
hawk had killed upon the snow. And I bethought
me that her whiteness was like that of the snow, and
that the blackness of her hair and her eyebrows was
like that of the raven, and that the two red spots
upon her cheeks were like the two drops of blood."
Said Gwalchmai, "This was not an ungentle thought,
and I should marvel if it were pleasant to thee to be
drawn from it." "Tell me," said Peredur, "is Kai
in Arthur's Court?" "He is," said he, "and behold
he is the knight that fought with thee last; and it
would have been better for him had he not come,
for his arm and his shoulder blade were broken with
the fall which he had from thy spear." "Verily,"
said Peredur, "I am not sorry to have thus begun to
avenge the insult to the dwarf and dwarfess." Then
Gwalchmai marvelled to hear him speak of the dwarf
and the dwarfess; and he approached him, and threw
his arms around his neck, and asked him what was
his name. "Peredur the son of Evrawc am I called,"
said he, "and thou? Who art thou?" "I am
called Gwalchmai," he replied. "I am right glad
to meet with thee," said Peredur, "for in every
country where I have been, I have heard of thy
fame for prowess and uprightness, and I solicit thy
fellowship." "Thou shalt have it, by my faith, and
grant me thine," said he. "Gladly will I do so,"
answered Peredur.

So they rode forth together joyfully towards the
place where Arthur was; and when Kai saw them

coming, he said, "I knew that Gwalchmai needed
not to fight the knight. And it is no wonder that
he should gain fame; more can he do by his fair
words, than I by the strength of my arm." And
Peredur went with Gwalchmai to his tent, and they
took off their armour. And Peredur put on garments
like those that Gwalchmai wore; and they went together unto Arthur, and saluted him. "Behold,
lord," said Gwalchmai, "him whom thou hast sought
so long." "Welcome unto thee, chieftain," said
Arthur. "With me thou shalt remain; and had I
known thy valour[1] had been such, thou shouldst
not have left me as thou didst. Nevertheless, this
was predicted of thee by the dwarf and the dwarfess,
whom Kai ill treated, and whom thou hast avenged."
And hereupon, behold there came the Queen and
her handmaidens, and Peredur saluted them. And
they were rejoiced to see him, and bade him welcome.
And Arthur did him great honour and respect, and
they returned towards Caerlleon.

And the first night, Peredur came to Caerlleon, to
Arthur's Court, and as he walked in the city after
his repast, behold, there met him Angharad Law
Eurawc. "By my faith, sister," said Peredur, "thou
art a beauteous and lovely maiden; and were it
pleasing to thee, I could love thee above all women."
"I pledge my faith," said she, "that I do not love
thee, nor will I ever do so." "I also pledge my
faith," said Peredur, "that I will never speak a word
to any Christian again, until thou come to love me
above all men."

The next day, Peredur went forth by the high road,
along a mountain ridge, and he saw a valley of a
circular form, the confines of which were rocky and

---

[1] Progress.

wooded. And the flat part of the valley was in meadows, and there were fields betwixt the meadows and the wood. And in the bosom of the wood he saw large black houses, of uncouth workmanship. And he dismounted, and led his horse towards the wood. And a little way within the wood he saw a rocky ledge, along which the road lay. And upon the ledge was a lion bound by a chain, and sleeping. And beneath the lion he saw a deep pit, of immense size, full of the bones of men and animals. And Peredur drew his sword, and struck the lion, so that he fell into the mouth of the pit, and hung there by the chain; and with a second blow he struck the chain, and broke it, and the lion fell into the pit, and Peredur led his horse over the rocky ledge, until he came into the valley. And in the centre of the valley he saw a fair castle, and he went towards it. And in the meadow by the Castle he beheld a huge grey man sitting, who was larger than any man he had ever before seen. And two young pages were shooting the hilts of their daggers, of the bone of the sea horse. And one of the pages had red hair, and the other auburn. And they went before him to the place where the grey man was. And Peredur saluted him. And the grey man said, " Disgrace to the beard of my porter." Then Peredur understood that the porter was the lion. And the grey man and the pages went together into the Castle, and Peredur accompanied them; and he found it a fair and noble place. And they proceeded to the hall, and the tables were already laid, and upon them was abundance of food and liquor.' And thereupon he saw an aged woman and a young woman come from the chamber; and they were the most stately women he had ever seen. Then they washed, and went to meat, and the grey

man sat in the upper seat at the head of the table,
and the aged woman next to him. And Peredur
and the maiden were placed together; and the two
young pages served them. And the maiden gazed
sorrowfully upon Peredur, and Peredur asked the
maiden wherefore she was sad. " For thee, my soul ;
for, from when I first beheld thee, I have loved
thee above all men. And it pains me to know that
so gentle a youth as thou should have such a doom
as awaits thee to-morrow. Sawest thou the numerous
black houses in the bosom of the wood. All these
belong to the vassals of the grey man yonder, who
is my father. And they are all giants. And to-
morrow they will rise up against thee, and will slay
thee. And the Round Valley is this valley called."
" Listen, fair maiden, wilt thou contrive that my
horse and arms be in 'the same lodging with me
to-night." " Gladly will I cause it so to be, by
Heaven, if I can."

And when it was time for them to sleep rather than
to carouse, they went to rest. And the maiden
caused Peredur's horse and arms to be in the same
lodging with him. And the next morning Peredur
heard a great tumult of men and horses around the
Castle. And Peredur arose, and armed himself and
his horse, and went to the meadow. Then the aged
woman and the maiden came to the grey man,
" Lord," said they, " take the word of the youth, that
he will never disclose what he has seen in this place,
and we will be his sureties that he keep it." " I will
not do so, by my faith," said the grey man. So
Peredur fought with the host; and towards evening,
he had slain the one-third of them without receiving
any hurt himself. Then said the aged woman, " Behold, many of thy host have been slain by the youth.

Do thou, therefore, grant him mercy." "I will not
grant it, by my faith," said he.   And the aged woman
and the fair maiden were upon the battlements of the
Castle, looking forth.   And at that juncture, Peredur
encountered the yellow-haired youth, and slew him.
"Lord," said the maiden, "grant the young man
mercy." "That will I not do, by Heaven," he
replied ; and thereupon Peredur attacked the auburn-
haired youth, and slew him likewise.   "It were better
thou hadst accorded mercy to the youth, before he
had slain thy two sons : for now scarcely wilt thou
thyself escape from him."   "Go, maiden, and beseech
the youth to grant mercy unto us, for we yield ourselves into his hands."   So the maiden came to the
place where Peredur was, and besought mercy for her
father, and for all such of his vassals as had escaped
alive.   "Thou shalt have it, on condition that thy
father, and all that are under him, go and render
homage to Arthur, and tell him that it was his vassal
Peredur that did him this service."   "This will we
do willingly, by Heaven."   "And you shall also
receive baptism ; and I will send to Arthur, and
beseech him to bestow this valley upon thee, and
upon thy heirs after thee for ever."   Then they went
in, and the grey man and the tall woman saluted
Peredur.   And the grey man said unto him, "Since
I have possessed this valley, I have not seen any
Christian depart with his life, save thyself.   And we
will go to do homage to Arthur, and to embrace the
faith, and be baptized."   Then said Peredur, "To
Heaven I render thanks that I have not broken my
vow to the lady that best I love, which was, that I
would not speak one word unto any Christian."

That night they tarried there.   And the next day,
in the morning, the grey man, with his company, set

forth to Arthur's Court; and they did homage unto
Arthur, and he caused them to be baptized. And
the grey man told Arthur, that it was Peredur that
had vanquished them. And Arthur gave the valley
to the grey man and his company, to hold it of
him as Peredur had besought. And with Arthur's
permission, the grey man went back to the Round
Valley.

Peredur rode forward next day, and he traversed a
vast tract of desert, in which no dwellings were. And
at length he came to a habitation, mean and small.
And there he heard that there was a serpent that lay
upon a gold ring, and suffered none to inhabit the
country for seven miles around. And Peredur came
to the place where he heard the serpent was. And
angrily, furiously, and desperately, fought he with the
serpent; and at the last he killed it, and took away
the ring. And thus he was for a long time without
speaking a word to any Christian. And therefrom he
lost his colour and his aspect, through extreme long-
ing after the Court of Arthur, and the society of the
lady whom best he loved, and of his companions.
Then he proceeded forward to Arthur's Court, and on
the road there met him Arthur's household, going on
a particular errand, with Kai at their head. And
Peredur knew them all, but none of the household
recognised him. " Whence comest thou, chieftain ? "
said Kai. And this he asked him twice, and three
times, and he answered him not. And Kai thrust
him through the thigh with his lance. And lest he
should be compelled to speak, and to break his vow,
he went on without stopping. " Then," said Gwalchmai, " I declare to Heaven, Kai, that thou hast acted
ill in committing such an outrage on a youth like this,
who cannot speak." And Gwalchmai returned back

to Arthur's Court. "Lady," said he to Gwenhwyvar, "seest thou how wicked an outrage Kai has committed upon this youth who cannot speak; for Heaven's sake, and for mine, cause him to have medical care before I come back, and I will repay thee the charge."

And before the men returned from their errand, a knight came to the meadow beside Arthur's Palace, to dare some one to the encounter. And his challenge was accepted; and Peredur fought with him, and overthrew him. And for a week he overthrew one knight every day.

And one day, Arthur and his household were going to Church, and they beheld a knight who had raised the signal for combat. "Verily," said Arthur, "by the valour of men, I will not go hence until I have my horse and my arms to overthrow yonder boor." Then went the attendants to fetch Arthur's horse and arms. And Peredur met the attendants as they were going back, and he took the horse and arms from them, and proceeded to the meadow; and all those who saw him arise and go to do battle with the knight, went upon the tops of the houses, and the mounds, and the high places, to behold the combat. And Peredur beckoned with his hand to the knight to commence the fight. And the knight thrust at him, but he was not thereby moved from where he stood. And Peredur spurred his horse, and ran at him wrathfully, furiously, fiercely, desperately, and with mighty rage, and he gave him a thrust, deadly-wounding, severe, furious, adroit and strong, under his jaw, and raised him out of his saddle, and cast him a long way from him. And Peredur went back, and left the horse and the arms with the attendant as before, and he went on foot to the Palace.

F

Then Peredur went by the name of the Dumb
Youth. And behold, Angharad Law Eurawc met
him. "I declare to Heaven, chieftain," said she,
"woeful is it that thou canst not speak; for couldst
thou speak, I would love thee best of all men; and,
by my faith, although thou canst not, I do love thee
above all." "Heaven reward thee, my sister," said
Peredur, "by my faith, I also do love thee." Thereupon it was known that he was Peredur. And then
he held fellowship with Gwalchmai, and Owain the
son of Urien, and all the household, and he remained
in Arthur's Court.

Arthur was in Caerlleon upon Usk; and he went
to hunt, and Peredur went with him. And Peredur
let loose his dog upon a hart, and the dog killed the
hart in a desert place. And a short space from him
he saw signs of a dwelling, and towards the dwelling
he went, and he beheld a hall, and at the door of the
hall he found bald swarthy youths playing at chess.
And when he entered, he beheld three maidens sitting
on a bench, and they were all clothed alike, as became
persons of high rank. And he came, and sat by them
upon the bench; and one of the maidens looked
steadfastly upon Peredur, and wept. And Peredur
asked her wherefore she was weeping. "Through
grief, that I should see so fair a youth as thou art,
slain." "Who will slay me?" enquired Peredur.
"If thou art so daring as to remain here to-night, I
will tell thee." "How great soever my danger may
be from remaining here, I will listen unto thee."
"This Palace is owned by him who is my father,
said the maiden, "and he slays every one who comes
hither without his leave." "What sort of a man is
thy father, that he is able to slay every one thus?"

"A man who does violence and wrong unto his neighbours, and who renders justice unto none." And hereupon he saw the youths arise and clear the chessmen from the board. And he heard a great tumult; and after the tumult there came in a huge black one-eyed man, and the maidens arose to meet him. And they disarrayed him, and he went and sat down; and after he had rested and pondered awhile, he looked at Peredur, and asked who the knight was. "Lord," said one of the maidens, "he is the fairest and gentlest youth that ever thou didst see. And for the sake of Heaven, and of thine own dignity, have patience with him." "For thy sake I will have patience, and I will grant him his life this night." Then Peredur came towards them to the fire, and partook of food and liquor, and entered into discourse with the ladies. And being elated with the liquor, he said to the black man, "It is a marvel to me, so mighty as thou sayest thou art, who could have put out thine eye?" "It is one of my habits," said the black man, "that whosoever puts to me the question which thou hast asked, shall not escape with his life, either as a free gift, or for a price." "Lord," said the maiden, "whatsoever he may say to thee in jest, and through the excitement of liquor, make good that which thou saidest and didst promise me just now." "I will do so, gladly, for thy sake," said he. "Willingly will I grant him his life this night." And that night thus they remained.

And the next day the black man got up, and put on his armour, and said to Peredur, "Arise, man, and suffer death." And Peredur said unto him, "Do one of two things, black man; if thou wilt fight with me, either throw off thy own armour, or give arms to me, that I may encounter thee." "Ha! man," said he, "couldst thou fight, if thou hadst arms? Take, then, what arms thou dost choose." And thereupon the maiden came to Peredur with such arms as pleased him; and he fought with the black man, and forced him to crave his mercy. "Black man, thou shalt have mercy, provided thou tell me who thou art, and who put out thine eye." "Lord, I will tell thee, I lost it in fighting with the Black Serpent of the Carn. There is a mound, which is called the Mound of Mourning; and on the mound there is a carn, and in the carn there is a serpent, and on the tail of the serpent there is a stone, and the virtues of the stone are such, that whosoever should hold it in one hand, in the other he will have as much gold as he may desire. And in fighting with this serpent was it that I lost my eye. And the Black Oppressor am I called. And for this reason I am called the Black Oppressor, that there is not a single man around me whom I have not oppressed, and justice have I done unto none." "Tell me" said Peredur, "how far is it hence?" "The same day that thou settest forth, thou wilt come to the Palace of the Sons of the King of the Tortures." "Wherefore are they called thus?" "The Addanc of the Lake slays them once every day. When thou goest thence, thou wilt come to the Court of the Countess of the Achievements." "What achievements are there?" asked Peredur. "Three hundred men there are in her household, and unto every stranger that comes to the Court, the achievements of her household are related. And this is the manner of it,—the three hundred men of the household sit next unto the Lady; and that not through disrespect unto the guests, but that they may relate the achievements of the household. And the day that thou goest thence, thou wilt reach the Mound of Mourning, and round

about the mound there are the owners of three
hundred tents guarding the serpent." " Since thou
hast, indeed, been an oppressor so long," said Peredur,
" I will cause that thou continue so no longer." So
he slew him.

Then the maiden spoke, and began to converse
with him. "If thou wast poor when thou camest
here, henceforth thou wilt be rich through the treasure
of the black man whom thou hast slain. Thou seest
the many lovely maidens that there are in this Court,
thou shalt have her whom thou best likest for the lady
of thy love." " Lady, I came not hither from my
country to woo ; but match yourselves as it liketh you
with the comely youths I see here ; and none of your
goods do I desire, for I need them not." Then
Peredur rode forward, and he came to the Palace of
the Sons of the King of the Tortures ; and when he
entered the Palace, he saw none but women ; and
they rose up, and were joyful at his coming ; and as
they began to discourse with him, he beheld a charger
arrive, with a saddle upon it, and a corpse in the
saddle. And one of the women arose, and took the
corpse from the saddle, and anointed it in a vessel of
warm water, which was below the door, and placed
precious balsam upon it ; and the man rose up alive,
and came to the place where Peredur was, and greeted
him, and was joyful to see him. And two other men
came in upon their saddles, and the maiden treated
these two in the same manner as she had done the
first. Then Peredur asked the chieftain wherefore it
was thus. And they told him, that there was an
Addanc in a cave, which slew them once every day.
And thus they remained that night.

And next morning the youths arose to sally forth,
and Peredur besought them, for the sake of the ladies

of their love, to permit him to go with them ; but they
refused him, saying, "If thou shouldst be slain there,
thou hast none to bring thee back to life again."
And they rode forward, and Peredur followed after
them ; and after they had disappeared out of his sight,
he came to a mound, whereon sat the fairest lady he
had ever beheld. "I know thy quest," said she,
" thou art going to encounter the Addanc, and he will
slay thee, and that not by courage, but by craft. He
has a cave, and at the entrance of the cave there is a
stone pillar, and he sees every one that enters, and
none see him ; and from behind the pillar he slays
every one with a poisonous dart. And if thou wouldst
pledge me thy faith, to love me above all women, I
would give thee a stone, by which thou shouldst see
him when thou goest in, and he should not see thee."
"I will, by my troth," said Peredur, "for when first
I beheld thee, I loved thee ; and where shall I seek
thee ?" "When thou seekest me, seek towards India."
And the maiden vanished, after placing the stone in
Peredur's hand.

And he came towards a valley, through which ran
a river ; and the borders of the valley were wooded,
and on each side of the river were level meadows.
And on one side of the river he saw a flock of white
sheep, and on the other a flock of black sheep. And
whenever one of the white sheep bleated, one of the
black sheep would cross over; and become white ; and
when one of the black sheep bleated, one of the white
sheep would cross over, and become black. And he
saw a tall tree by the side of the river, one half of
which was in flames from the root to the top, and the
other half was green and in full leaf. And nigh
thereto he saw a youth sitting upon a mound, and two
greyhounds, white-breasted, and spotted, in leashes,

lying by his side. And certain was he, that he had never seen a youth of so royal a bearing as he. And in the wood opposite he heard hounds raising a herd of deer. And Peredur· saluted the youth, and the youth greeted him in return. And there were three roads leading from the mound; two of them were wide roads, and the third was more narrow. And Peredur enquired where the three roads went. " One of them goes to my palace," said the youth, "and one of two things I counsel thee to do, either to proceed to my palace, which is before thee, and where thou wilt find my wife, or else to remain here to see the hounds chasing the roused deer from the wood to the plain. And thou shalt see the best greyhounds thou didst ever behold, and the boldest in the chase, kill them by the water beside us; and when it is time to go to meat, my page will come with my horse to meet me, and thou shalt rest in my palace to-night." " Heaven reward thee; but I cannot tarry, for onward must I go." "The other road leads to the town, which is near here, and wherein food and liquor may be bought; and the road which is narrower than the others goes towards the cave of the Addanc." "With thy permission, young man, I will go that way,"

And Peredur went towards the cave. And he took the stone in his left hand, and his lance in his right. And as he went in, he perceived the Addanc, and he pierced him through with his lance, and cut off his head. And as he came from the cave, behold the three companions were at the entrance; and they saluted Peredur, and told him that there was a pre · diction that he should slay that monster. And Peredur gave the head to the young men, and they offered him in marriage whichever of the three sisters

he might choose, and half their kingdom with her.
"I came not hither to woo," said Peredur, "but if
peradventure I took a wife, I should prefer your sister
to all others." And Peredur rode forward, and he
heard a noise behind him. And he looked back, and
saw a man upon a red horse, with red armour upon
him; and the man rode up by his side, and saluted
him, and wished him the favour of Heaven and of
man. And Peredur greeted the youth kindly.
"Lord, I come to make a request unto thee."
"What wouldest thou?" "That thou shouldest take
me as thine attendant." "Who then should I take
as my attendant, if I did so?" "I will not conceal
from thee what kindred I am of. Etlym Gleddyv
Coch am I called, an Earl from the East Country."
"I marvel that thou shouldest offer to become attendant to a man whose possessions are no greater than
thine own; for I have but an earldom like thyself.
But since thou desirest to be my attendant, I will take
thee joyfully."

And they went forward to the Court of the Countess,
and all they of the Court were glad at their coming;
and they were told it was not through disrespect they
were placed below the household, but that such was
the usage of the Court. For, whoever should overthrow the three hundred men of her household, would
sit next the Countess, and she would love him above
all men. And Peredur having overthrown the three
hundred men of her household, sat down beside her,
and the Countess said, "I thank Heaven that I have
a youth so fair and so valiant as thou, since I have
not obtained the man whom best I love." "Who is
he whom best thou lovest?" "By my faith, Etlym
Gleddyv Coch is the man whom I love best, and I
have never seen him." "Of a truth, Etlym is my

companion; and behold here he is, and for his sake
did I come to joust with thy household. And he
could have done so better than I, had it pleased him.
And I do give thee unto him." "Heaven reward
thee, fair youth, and I will take the man whom I love
above all others." And the Countess became Etlym's
bride from that moment.

And the next day Peredur set forth towards the
Mound of Mourning. "By thy hand, lord, but I will
go with thee," said Etlym. Then they went forwards
till they came in sight of the mound and the tents.
"Go unto yonder men," said Peredur to Etlym, "and
desire them to come and do me homage." So Etlym
went unto them, and said unto them thus—"Come
and do homage to my lord." "Who is thy lord?"
said they. "Peredur with the long lance is my lord,"
said Etlym. "Were it permitted to slay a messenger,
thou shouldest not go back to thy lord alive, for
making unto Kings, and Earls, and Barons, so
arrogant a demand as to. go and do him homage."
Peredur desired him to go back to them, and to give
them their choice, either to do him homage or to do
battle with him. And they chose rather to do battle.
And that day Peredur overthrew the owners of a
hundred tents. - And the next day he overthrew the
owners of a hundred more; and the third day the
remaining hundred took counsel to do homage to
Peredur. And Peredur enquired of them, wherefore
they were there. And they told him they were guarding the serpent until he should die. "For then
should we fight for the stone among ourselves, and
whoever should be conqueror among us would have
the stone." "Await here," said Peredur, "and I will
go to encounter the serpent." "Not so, lord," said
they, "we will go altogether to encounter the serpent."

" Verily," said Peredur, "that will I not permit; for if the serpent be slain, I shall derive no more fame therefrom than one of you." Then he went to the place where the serpent was, and slew it, and came back to them, and said, " Reckon up what you have spent since you have been here, and I will repay you to the full." And he paid to each what he said was his claim. And he required of them only that they should acknowledge themselves his vassals. And he said to Etlym, " Go back unto her whom thou lovest best, and I will go forwards, and I will reward thee for having been my attendant." And he gave Etlym the stone. " Heaven repay thee and prosper thee," said Etlym.

And Peredur rode thence, and he came to the fairest valley he had ever seen, through which ran a river; and there he beheld many tents of various colours. And he marvelled still more at the number of water-mills and of wind-mills that he saw. And there rode up with him a tall auburn-haired man, in a workman's garb, and Peredur enquired of him who he was. " I am the chief miller," said he, " of all the mills yonder." " Wilt thou give me lodging ? " said Peredur. " I will, gladly," he answered. And Peredur came to the miller's house, and the miller had a fair and pleasant dwelling. And Peredur asked money as a loan from the miller, that he might buy meat and liquor for himself, and for the household, and he promised that he would pay him again ere he went thence. And he enquired of the miller, wherefore such a multitude were there assembled. Said the miller to Peredur, " One thing is certain ; either thou art a man from afar, or thou art beside thyself. The Empress of Cristinobyl the Great is here ; and she will have no one but the man who is most valiant ;

for riches does she not require. And it was impossible to bring food for so many thousands as are
here, therefore were all these mills constructed."
And that night they took their rest.

And the next day Peredur arose, and he equipped
himself and his horse for the tournament. And
among the other tents, he beheld one, which was
the fairest he had ever seen. And he saw a beauteous
maiden leaning her head out of a window of the tent,
and he had never seen a maiden more lovely than
she. And upon her was a garment of satin. And he
gazed fixedly on the maiden, and began to love her
greatly. And he remained there, gazing upon the
maiden from morning until mid-day, and from mid-
day until evening; and then the tournament was
ended ; and he went to his lodging, and drew off his
armour. Then he asked money of the miller as a
loan, and the miller's wife was wroth with Peredur ;
nevertheless, the miller lent him the money. And
the next day he did in like manner as he had done
the day before. And at night he came to his lodging,
and took money as a loan from the miller. And the
third day, as he was in the same place, gazing upon
the maiden, he felt a hard blow between the neck and
the shoulder, from the edge of an axe. And when he
looked behind him, he saw that it was the miller;
and the miller said to him, " Do one of two things :
either turn thy head from hence, or go to the tournament." And Peredur smiled on the miller, and
went to the tournament ; and all that encountered
him that day, he overthrew. And as many as he
vanquished, he sent as a gift to the Empress, and
their horses and arms he sent as a gift to the wife of
the miller, in payment of the borrowed money.
Peredur attended the tournament until all were over-

thrown, and he sent all the men to the prison of the
Empress, and the horses and arms to the wife of the
miller, in payment of the borrowed money.   And the
Empress sent to the Knight of the Mill, to ask him
to come and visit her.   And Peredur went not for
the first nor for the second message.   And the third
time she sent an hundred knights to bring him
against his will, and they went to him, and told him
their mission from the Empress.   And Peredur
fought well with them, and caused them to be bound
like stags, and thrown into the mill dyke.   And the
Empress sought advice of a wise man, who was in
her counsel; and he said to her, "With thy permission, I will go to him myself."   So he came to
Peredur, and saluted him, and besought him, for the
sake of the lady of his love, to come and visit the
Empress.   And they went, together with the miller.
And Peredur went and sat down in the outer chamber
of the tent, and she came and placed herself by his
side.   And there was but little discourse between them.
And Peredur took his leave, and went to his lodging.

   And the next day he came to visit her, and when
he came into the tent, there was no one chamber less
decorated than the others.   And they knew not where
he would sit.   And Peredur went and sat beside the
Empress, and discoursed with her courteously.   And
while they were thus, they beheld a black man enter
with a goblet full of wine in his hand.   And he
dropped upon his knee before the Empress, and
besought her to give it to no one who would not
fight with him for it.   And she looked upon Peredur.
"Lady," said he, "bestow on me the goblet."   And
Peredur drank the wine, and gave the goblet to the
miller's wife.   And while they were thus, behold
there entered a black man, of larger stature than the

other, with a wild beast's claw in his hand, wrought
into the form of a goblet, and filled with wine. And
he presented it to the Empress, and besought her to
give it to no one but the man who would fight with
him. "Lady," said Peredur, "bestow it on me."
And she gave it to him. And Peredur drank the
wine, and sent the goblet to the wife of the miller.
And while they were thus, behold a rough-looking
crisp-haired man, taller than either of the others, came
in with a bowl in his hand full of wine; and he bent
upon his knee, and gave it into the hands of the
Empress, and he besought her to give it to none but
him who would fight with him for it; and she gave
it to Peredur, and he sent it to the miller's wife.
And that night Peredur returned to his lodging; and
the next day he accoutred himself and his horse, and
went to the meadow, and slew the three men. Then
Peredur proceeded to the tent, and the Empress said
to him, "Goodly Peredur, remember the faith thou
didst pledge me when I gave thee the stone, and thou
didst kill the Addanc." "Lady," answered he, "thou
sayest truth, I do remember it." And Peredur was
entertained by the Empress fourteen years, as the
story relates.

Arthur was at Caerlleon upon Usk, his principal
palace; and in the centre of the floor of the hall were
four men sitting on a carpet of velvet, Owain the son
of Urien, and Gwalchmai the son of Gwyar, and
Howel the son of Emyr Llydaw, and Peredur of the
long lance. And thereupon they saw a black curly-
headed maiden enter, riding upon a yellow mule, with
jagged thongs in her hand, to urge it on; and having
a rough and hideous aspect. Blacker were her face
and her two hands than the blackest iron covered

with pitch ; and her hue was not more frightful than
her form.   High cheeks had she, and a face lengthened
downwards, and a short nose with distended nostrils.
And one eye was of a piercing mottled grey, and the
other was as black as jet, deep sunk in her head.
And her teeth were long and yellow, more yellow were
they than the flower of the broom.   And her stomach
rose from the breast bone, higher than her chin.
And her back was in the shape of a crook, and her
legs were large and bony.   And her figure was very
thin and spare, except her feet and her legs, which
were of huge size.   And she greeted Arthur and all
his household, except Peredur.   And to Peredur she
spoke harsh and angry words.   " Peredur, I greet thee
not, seeing that thou dost not merit it.   Blind was
fate in giving thee fame and favour.   When thou wast
in the Court of the Lame King, and didst see there
the youth bearing the streaming spear, from the points
of which were drops of blood flowing in streams, even
to the hand of the youth, and many other wonders
likewise, thou didst not enquire their meaning nor
their cause.   Hadst thou done so, the King would
have been restored to health, and his dominions to
peace.   Whereas, from henceforth, he will have to
endure battles and conflicts, and his knights will
perish, and wives will be widowed, and maidens will
be left portionless, and all this is because of thee."
Then said she unto Arthur, " May it please thee, lord,
my dwelling is far hence, in the stately castle of which
thou hast heard, and therein are five hundred and
sixty-six knights of the order of Chivalry, and the lady
whom best he loves with each ; and whoever would
acquire fame in arms, and encounters, and conflicts,
he will gain it there, if he deserve it.   And whoso
would reach the summit of fame and of honour, I

know where he may find it.   There is a Castle on a
lofty mountain, and there is a maiden therein, and
she is detained a prisoner there, and whoever shall
set her free will attain the summit of the fame of the
world."   And thereupon she rode away.

Said Gwalchmai, "By my faith, I will not rest
tranquilly until I have proved if I can release the
maiden."   And many of Arthur's household joined
themselves with him.   Then, likewise said Peredur,
"By my faith, I will not rest tranquilly until I know
the story and meaning of the lance whereof the black
maiden spoke."   And while they were equipping
themselves, behold a knight came to the gate.   And
he had the size and the strength of a warrior, and was
equipped with arms and habiliments.   And he went
forward, and saluted Arthur and all his household,
except Gwalchmai.   And the knight had upon his
shoulder a shield, ingrained with gold, with a fesse
of azure blue upon it, and his whole armour was of
the same hue.   And he said to Gwalchmai, " Thou
didst slay my lord, by thy treachery and deceit, and
that will I prove upon thee."   Then Gwalchmai rose
up.   "Behold," said he, "here is my gage against
thee, to maintain either in this place, or wherever else
thou wilt, that I am not a traitor or deceiver."
"Before the King whom I obey, will I that my
encounter with thee take place," said the knight.
"Willingly," said Gwalchmai, "go forward, and I will
follow thee."   So the knight went forth, and Gwalchmai accoutred himself, and there was offered unto him
abundance of armour, but he would take none but
his own.   And when Gwalchmai and Peredur were
equipped, they set forth to follow him, by reason of
their fellowship, and of the great friendship that was
between them.   And they did not go after him

in company together, but each went his own
way.

At the dawn of day, Gwalchmai came to a valley,
and in the valley he saw a fortress, and within the
fortress a vast palace, and lofty towers around it. And
he beheld a knight coming out to hunt from the other
side, mounted on a spirited black snorting palfrey,
that advanced at a prancing pace, proudly stepping,
and nimbly bounding, and sure of foot; and this was
the man to whom the palace belonged. And Gwalchmai saluted him, " Heaven prosper thee, chieftain,"
said he, " and whence comest thou?" "I come,"
answered he, " from the Court of Arthur." " And
art thou Arthur's vassal?" " Yes, by my faith," said
Gwalchmai. " I will give thee good counsel," said
the knight. " I see that thou art tired and weary, go
unto my palace, if it may please thee, and tarry there
to-night." " Willingly, lord," said he, " and Heaven
reward thee." " Take this ring as a token to the
porter, and go forward to yonder tower, and therein
thou wilt find my sister." And Gwalchmai went to
the gate, and shewed the ring, and proceeded to the
tower. And on entering, he beheld a large blazing
fire, burning without smoke, and with a bright and
lofty flame, and a beauteous and stately maiden was
sitting on a chair by the fire. And the maiden was
glad at his coming, and welcomed him, and advanced
to meet him. And he went and sat beside the maiden,
and they took their repast. And when their repast
was over, they discoursed pleasantly together. And
while they were thus, behold there entered a venerable
hoary-headed man. " Ah! base girl," said he, " if
thou didst think that it was right for thee to entertain
and to sit by yonder man; thou wouldest not do so."
And he withdrew his head, and went forth. " Ha!

chieftain," said the maiden, "if thou wilt do as I counsel thee, thou wilt shut the door, lest the man should have a plot against thee." Upon that Gwalchmai arose, and when he came near unto the door, the man, with sixty others, fully armed, were ascending the tower. And Gwalchmai defended the door with a chess-board, that none might enter until the man should return from the chase. And thereupon, behold the earl arrived. "What is all this?" asked he. "It is a sad thing," said the hoary-headed man, "the young girl yonder has been sitting and eating with him who slew your father. He is Gwalchmai the son of Gwyar." "Hold thy peace, then," said the earl, "I will go in." And the earl was joyful concerning Gwalchmai. "Ha! chieftain," said he, "it was wrong of thee to come to my Court, when thou knewest that thou didst slay my father; and though we cannot avenge him, Heaven will avenge him upon thee." "My soul," said Gwalchmai, "thus it is; I came not here either to acknowledge or to deny having slain thy father; but I am on a message from Arthur, and therefore do I crave the space of a year until I shall return from my embassy, and then, upon my faith, I will come back unto this palace, and do one of two things, either acknowledge it, or deny it." And the time was granted him willingly; and he remained there that night. And the next morning he rode forth. And the story relates nothing further of Gwalchmai respecting this adventure.

And Peredur rode forward. And he wandered over the whole island, seeking tidings of the black maiden, and he could meet with none. And he came to an unknown land, in the centre of a valley, watered by a river. And as he traversed the valley, he beheld a horseman coming towards him, and wearing the

G

garments of a priest, and he besought his blessing.
"Wretched man," said he, "thou meritest no blessing,
and thou wouldst not be profited by one, seeing that
thou art clad in armour on such a day as this."
"And what day is to-day?" said Peredur. "To-day
is Good Friday," he answered. "Chide me not, that
I knew not this, seeing that it is a year to-day since I
journeyed forth from my country." Then he dismounted, and led his horse in his hand. And he had
not proceeded far along the high road before he came
to a cross road, and the cross road traversed a wood.
And on the other side of the wood he saw an un-
fortified castle, which appeared to be inhabited. And
at the gate of the castle there met him the priest
whom he had seen before, and he asked his blessing.
"The blessing of Heaven be unto thee," said he, "it
is more fitting to travel in thy present guise, than as
thou wast crewhile; and this night thou shalt tarry
with me." So he remained there that night.

And the next day Peredur sought to go forth.
"To-day may no one journey. Thou shalt remain
with me to-day and to-morrow, and the day following,
and I will direct thee as best I may to the place which
thou art seeking." And the fourth day Peredur
sought to go forth, and he entreated the priest to tell
him how he should find the Castle of Wonders.
"What I know thereof, I will tell thee," he replied.
"Go over yonder mountain, and on the other side of
the mountain thou wilt come to a river, and in the
valley wherein the river runs is a King's Palace,
wherein the King sojourned during Easter. And if
thou mayest have tidings anywhere of the Castle of
Wonders, thou wilt have them there."

Then Peredur rode forward. And he came to the
valley in which was the river, and there met him a

number of men going to hunt, and in the midst of
them was a man of exalted rank, and Peredur saluted
him. "Choose, chieftain," said the man, "whether
thou wilt go with me to the chase, or wilt proceed to
my Palace, and I will despatch one of my household
to commend thee to my daughter, who is there, and
who will entertain thee with food and liquor until I
return from hunting; and whatever may be thine
errand, such as I can obtain for thee, thou shalt
gladly have." And the King sent a little yellow page
with him as an attendant; and when they came to
the palace, the lady had arisen, and was about to wash
before meat. Peredur went forward, and she saluted
him joyfully, and placed him by her side. And they
took their repast. And whatsoever Peredur said unto
her, she laughed loudly, so that all in the palace could
hear. Then spoke the yellow page to the lady. "By
my faith," said he, "this youth is already thy husband;
or if he be not, thy mind and thy thoughts are set
upon him." And the little yellow page went unto the
King, and told him that it seemed to him that the
youth whom he had met with was his daughter's
husband, or if he were not so already, that he would
shortly become so, unless he were cautious. "What
is thy counsel in this matter, youth?" said the King.
"My counsel is," he replied, "that thou set strong
men upon him, to seize him, until thou hast ascer-
tained the truth respecting this." So he set strong
men upon Peredur, who seized him, and cast him
into prison. And the maiden went before her father,
and asked him, wherefore he had caused the youth
from Arthur's Court to be imprisoned. "In truth,"
he answered, "he shall not be free to-night, nor to-
morrow, nor the day following, and he shall not come
from where he is." She replied not to what the king

had said, but she went to the youth. "Is it unpleasant to thee to be here?" said she. "I should not care, if I were not," he replied." "Thy couch and thy treatment shall be in no wise inferior to that of the King himself, and thou shalt have the best entertainment that the palace affords. And if it were more pleasing to thee that my couch should be here, that I might discourse with thee, it should be so, cheerfully." "This can I not refuse," said Peredur. And he remained in prison that night. And the maiden provided all that she had promised him.

And the next day Peredur heard a tumult in the town. "Tell me, fair maiden, what is that tumult?" said Peredur. "All the King's hosts and his forces have come to the town to-day." "And what seek they here?" he enquired. "There is an Earl near this place, who possesses two Earldoms, and is as powerful as a king; and an engagement will take place between them to-day." "I beseech thee," said Peredur, "to cause a horse and arms to be brought, that I may view the encounter, and I promise to come back to my prison again." "Gladly," said she, "will I provide thee with horse and arms." So she gave him a horse and arms, and a bright scarlet robe of honour over his armour, and a yellow shield upon his shoulder. And he went to the combat; and as many of the Earl's men as encountered him that day, he overthrew; and he returned to his prison. And the maiden asked tidings of Peredur, and he answered her not a word. And she went and asked tidings of her father, and enquired who had acquitted himself best of the household. And he said that he knew not, but that it was a man with a scarlet robe of honour over his armour, and a yellow shield upon his shoulder. Then she smiled, and returned to where

Peredur was, and did him great honour that night.
And for three days did Peredur slay the Earl's men ;
and before any one could know who he was, he
returned to his prison. And the fourth day Peredur
slew the Earl himself. And the maiden went unto
her father, and enquired of him the news. "I have
good news for thee," said the King, "the Earl is slain,
and I am the owner of his two Earldoms." "Knowest
thou, lord, who slew him?" "I do not know," said
the King. "It was the knight with the scarlet robe
of honour, and the yellow shield." "Lord," said she,
"I know who that is." "By Heaven," he exclaimed,
"who is he?" "Lord," she replied, "he is the
knight whom thou hast imprisoned." Then he went
unto Peredur, and saluted him, and told him that he
would reward the service he had done him, in any
way he might desire. And when they went to meat,
Peredur was placed beside the King, and the maiden
on the other side of Peredur, "I will give thee,"
said the King, "my daughter in marriage, and half
my kingdom with her, and the two Earldoms as a
gift." "Heaven reward thee, lord," said Peredur,
"but I came not here to woo." "What seekest thou,
then, chieftain?" "I am seeking tidings of the Castle
of Wonders." "Thy enterprise is greater, chieftain,
than thou wilt wish to pursue," said the maiden,
"nevertheless, tidings shalt thou have of the Castle,
and thou shalt have a guide through my father's
dominions, and a sufficiency of provisions for thy
journey, for thou art, O chieftain, the man whom best
I love." Then she said to him, "Go over yonder
mountain, and thou wilt find a Lake, and in the
middle of the Lake there is a Castle, and that is the
Castle that is called the Castle of Wonders ; and we

know not what wonders are therein, but thus is it
called."

And Peredur proceeded towards the Castle, and the
gate of the Castle was open. And when he came to
the hall, the door was open, and he entered. And he
beheld a chessboard in the hall, and the chessmen
were playing against each other, by themselves. And
the side that he favoured lost the game,[1] and thereupon the others set up a shout, as though they had
been living men. And Peredur was wroth, and took
the chessmen in his lap, and cast the chessboard into
the lake. And when he had done thus, behold the
black maiden came in, and she said to him, "The
welcome of Heaven be not unto thee. Thou hadst
rather do evil than good." "What complaint hast
thou against me, maiden?" said Peredur. "That
thou hast occasioned unto the Empress the loss of her
chessboard, which she would not have lost for all her
empire. And the way in which thou mayest recover
the chessboard is, to repair to the Castle of Ysbidinongyl, where is a black man, who lays waste the
dominions of the Empress; and if thou canst slay
him, thou wilt recover the chessboard. But if thou
goest there, thou wilt not return alive." "Wilt thou
direct me thither?" said Peredur. "I will show thee
the way," she replied. So he went to the Castle of
Ysbidinongyl, and he fought with the black man.
And the black man besought mercy of Peredur.
"Mercy will I grant thee," said he, "on condition
that thou cause the chessboard to be restored to the
place where it was when I entered the hall." Then
the maiden came to him and said, "The malediction
of Heaven attend thee for thy work, since thou hast
left that monster alive, who lays waste all the posses-

---

[1] And the side that he would favour would lose the game.

sions of the Empress." "I granted him his life," said Peredur, "that he might cause the chessboard to be restored." "The chessboard is not in the place where thou didst find it; go back, therefore, and slay him," answered she. So Peredur went back, and slew the black man. And when he returned to the palace, he found the black maiden there. "Ah! maiden," said Peredur, "where is the Empress?" "I declare to Heaven that thou wilt not see her now, unless thou dost slay the monster that is in yonder forest." "What monster is there?" "It is a stag that is as swift as the swiftest bird; and he has one horn in his forehead, as long as the shaft of a spear and as sharp as whatever is sharpest. And he destroys the branches of the best trees in the forest and he kills every animal that he meets with therein; and those that he does not slay perish of hunger. And what is worse than that, he comes every night, and drinks up the fish pond, and leaves the fishes exposed, so that for the most part they die before the water returns again." "Maiden," said Peredur, "wilt thou come and show me this animal?" "Not so," said the maiden, "for he has not permitted any mortal to enter the forest for above a twelvemonth. Behold, here is a little dog belonging to the Empress, which will rouse the stag, and will chase him towards thee, and the stag will attack thee." Then the little dog went as a guide to Peredur, and roused the stag, and brought him towards the place where Peredur was. And the stag attacked Peredur, and he let him pass by him, and as he did so, he smote off his head with his sword. And while he was looking at the head of the stag, he saw a lady on horseback coming towards him. And she took the little dog in the lappet of her cap, and the head and the body of the

stag lay before her.   And around the stag's neck was
a golden collar.   "Ha! chieftain," said she, "uncourteously hast thou acted in slaying the fairest jewel
that was in my dominions."   "I was intreated so to
do ; and is there any way by which I can obtain thy
friendship ? "   "There is," she replied.   "Go thou
forward unto yonder mountain, and there thou wilt
find a grove ; and in the grove there is a cromlech,
do thou there challenge a man three times to fight,
and thou shalt have my friendship."

So Peredur proceeded onward, and came to the side
of the grove, and challenged any man to fight.   And
a black man arose from beneath the cromlech,
mounted upon a bony horse, and both he and his
horse were clad in huge rusty armour.   And they
fought.   And as often as Peredur cast the black man
to the earth, he would jump again into his saddle.
And Peredur dismounted, and drew his sword ; and
thereupon the black man disappeared with Peredur's
horse and his own, so that he could not gain sight of
him a second time.   And Peredur went along the
mountain, and on the other side of the mountain he
beheld a castle in the valley, wherein was a river.
And he went to the castle ; and as he entered it, he
saw a hall, and the door of the hall was open, and he
went in.   And there he saw a lame grey-headed man,
sitting on one side of the hall, with Gwalchmai beside
him.   And Peredur beheld his horse, which the black
man had taken, in the same stall with that of Gwalchmai.   And they were glad concerning Peredur.   And
he went and seated himself on the other side of the
hoary-headed man.   Then, behold a yellow-haired
youth came, and bent upon the knee before Peredur,
and besought his friendship.   " Lord," said the youth,
" it was I that came in the form of the black maiden

to Arthur's Court, and when thou didst throw down
the chessboard, and when thou didst slay the black
man of Ysbidinongyl, and when thou didst slay the
stag, and when thou didst go to fight the black man
of the cromlech. And I came with the bloody head
in the salver, and with the lance that streamed with
blood from the point to the hand, all along the shaft;
and the head was thy cousin's, and he was killed by
the sorceresses of Gloucester, who also lamed thine
uncle; and I am thy cousin. And there is a pre-

diction that thou art to avenge these things." Then
Peredur and Gwalchmai took counsel, and sent to
Arthur and his household, to beseech them to come
against the sorceresses. And they began to fight with
them, and one of the sorceresses slew one of Arthur's
men before Peredur's face, and Peredur bade her for-
bear. And the sorceress slew a man before Peredur's
face a second time, and a second time he forbade her.
And the third time the sorceress slew a man before

the face of Peredur, and then Peredur drew his sword, and smote the sorceress on the helmet ; and all her head armour was split in two parts. And she set up a cry, and desired the other sorceresses to flee, and told them that this was Peredur, the man who had learnt Chivalry with them, and by whom they were destined to be slain. Then Arthur and his household fell upon the sorceresses, and slew the sorceresses of Gloucester every one. And thus is it related concerning the Castle of Wonders.

HERE IS THE STORY OF
LLUDD AND LLEVELYS.

BELI THE GREAT, the son of Manogan, had three sons,
Lludd, and Caswallawn, and Nynyaw; and according to the story he had a fourth son called Llevelys.
And after the death of Beli, the kingdom of the
Island of Britain fell into the hands of Lludd his
eldest son; and Lludd ruled prosperously, and re-
built the walls of London, and encompassed it about

with numberless towers. And after that he bade the
citizens build houses therein, such as no houses in
the kingdom could equal. And moreover he was a
mighty warrior, and generous and liberal in giving
meat and drink to all that sought them. And though
he had many castles and cities, this one loved he
more than any. And he dwelt therein most part of
the year, and therefore was it called Caer Ludd, and
at last Caer London. And after the stranger-race
came there, it was called London, or Lwndrys.

Lludd loved Llevelys best of all his brothers,
because he was a wise and a discreet man. Having
heard that the king of France had died, leaving no
heir, except a daughter, and that he had left all his
possessions in her hands, he came to Lludd his
brother, to beseech his counsel and aid. And that
not so much for his own welfare, as to seek to add
to the glory and honour and dignity of his kindred, if
he might go to France to woo the maiden for his
wife. And forthwith his brother conferred with him,
and this counsel was pleasing unto him.

So he prepared ships and filled them with armed
knights, and set forth towards France. And as soon
as they had landed, they sent messengers to show the
nobles of France the cause of the embassy. And by
the joint counsel of the nobles of France and of the
princes, the maiden was given to Llevelys, and the
crown of the kingdom with her. And thenceforth he
ruled the land discreetly, and wisely, and happily, as
long as his life lasted.

After a space of time had passed, three plagues fell
on the Island of Britain, such as none in the Islands
had ever seen the like. The first was a certain race
that came, and was called the Çoranians; and so

great was their knowledge, that there was no discourse upon the face of the Island, however low it might be spoken, but what, if the wind met it, it was known to them. And through this they could not be injured.

The second plague was a shriek which came on every May eve, over every hearth in the Island of Britain. And this went through people's hearts, and so scared them, that the men lost their hue and their strength, and the women their children, and the young men, and the maidens lost their senses, and all the animals and trees and the earth and the waters, were left barren.

The third plague was, that however much of provisions and food might be prepared in the king's courts, were there even so much as a year's provision of meat and drink, none of it could ever be found, except what was consumed in the first night. And two of these plagues, no one ever knew their cause, therefore was there better hope of being freed from the first than from the second and third.

And thereupon King Lludd felt great sorrow and care, because that he knew not how he might be freed from these plagues. And he called to him all the nobles of his kingdom, and asked counsel of them what they should do against these afflictions. And by the common counsel of the nobles, Lludd the son of Beli, went to Llevelys his brother, king of France, for he was a man great of counsel and wisdom, to seek his advice.

And they made ready a fleet, and that in secret and in silence, lest that race should know the cause of their errand, or any besides the king and his counsellors. And when they were made ready, they went into their ships, Lludd and those whom he chose with him.   And they began to cleave the seas towards France.

And when these tidings came to Llevelys, seeing that he knew not the cause of his brother's ships, he came on the other side to meet him, and with him was a fleet vast of size.   And when Lludd saw this, he left all the ships out upon the sea except one only ; and in that one he came to meet his brother, and he likewise with a single ship came to meet him.   And when they were come together, each put his arms about the other's neck, and they welcomed each other with brotherly love.

After that Lludd had shewn his brother the cause of his errand, Llevelys said that he himself knew the cause of the coming to those lands.   And they took counsel together to discourse [1] on the matter otherwise than thus, in order that the wind might not catch their words, nor the Coranians know what they might say.   Then Llevelys caused a long horn to be made of brass, and through this horn they discoursed.   But whatsoever words they spoke through this horn, one to the other, neither of them could hear any other but harsh and hostile words.   And when Llevelys saw this, and that there was a demon thwarting them and disturbing through this horn, he caused wine to be put therein to wash it.   And through the virtue of the wine the demon was driven out of the horn. And when their discourse was unobstructed, Llevelys told his brother that he would give him some insects, whereof he should keep some to breed, lest by chance the like affliction might come a second time. And other of these insects he should take and bruise in water.   And he assured him that it would have

[1] Add " henceforth."

power to destroy the race of the Coranians. That is to say, that when he came home to his kingdom he should call together all the people both of his own race and of the race of the Coranians for a conference, as though with the intent of making peace between them; and that when they were all together, he should take this charmed water, and cast it over all alike. And he assured him that the water would

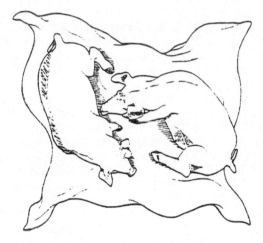

poison the race of the Coranians, but that it would not slay or harm those of his own race.

"And the second plague," said he, "that is in thy dominion, behold it is a dragon. And another dragon of a foreign race is fighting with it, and striving to overcome it. And therefore does your dragon make a fearful outcry. And on this wise mayest thou come to know this. After thou hast returned home, cause the Island to be measured in its length and breadth, and in the place where thou dost find the exact central point, there cause a pit to be dug, and cause a cauldron, full of the best mead that can be made, to be put in the pit, with a covering of satin over the face of the cauldron. And then, in thine own person do thou remain there watching, and thou wilt see the dragons fighting in the form of terrific animals. And at length they will take the form of dragons in the air. And last of all, after wearying themselves with fierce and furious fighting, they will fall in the form of two pigs upon the covering, and they will sink in, and the covering with them, and they will draw it down to the very bottom of the cauldron. And they will drink up the whole of the mead ; and after that they will sleep. Thereupon do thou immediately fold the covering around them, and bury them in a kistvaen, in the strongest place thou hast in thy dominions, and hide them in the earth. And as long as they shall bide in that strong place, no plague shall come to the Island of Britain from elsewhere.

"The cause of the third plague," said he, "is a mighty man of magic, who takes thy meat and thy drink and thy store. And he through illusions and charms causes every one to sleep. Therefore it is needful for thee in thy own person to watch thy food and thy provisions. And lest he should overcome thee with sleep, be there a cauldron of cold water by thy side, and when thou art oppressed with sleep, plunge into the cauldron."

Then Lludd returned back unto his land. And immediately he summoned to him the whole of his own race and of the Coranians. And as Llevelys had taught him, he bruised the insects in water, the

H

which he cast over them all together, and forthwith it destroyed the whole tribe of the Coranians, without hurt to any of the Britons.

And some time after this Lludd caused the Island to be measured in its length and in its breadth. And in Oxford he found the central point, and in that place he caused the earth to be dug, and in that pit a cauldron to be set, full of the best mead that could be made, and a covering of satin over the face of it. And he himself watched that night. And while he was there, he beheld the dragons fighting. And when they were weary they fell, and came down upon the top of the satin, and drew it with them to the bottom of the cauldron. And when they had drunk the mead they slept. And in their sleep, Lludd folded the covering around them, and in the securest place he had in Snowdon, he hid them in a kistvaen. Now after that this spot was called Dinas Emreis, but before that, Dinas Ffaraon. And thus the fierce outcry ceased in his dominions.

And when this was ended, King Lludd caused an exceeding great banquet to be prepared. And when it was ready, he placed a vessel of cold water by his side, and he in his own proper person watched it. And as he abode thus clad with arms, about the third watch of the night, lo! he heard many surpassing fascinations and various songs. And drowsiness urged him to sleep. Upon this, lest he should be hindered from his purpose and be overcome by sleep, he went often into the water. And at last, behold, a man of vast size, clad in strong, heavy armour, came in, bearing a hamper. And, as he was wont, he put all the food and provisions of meat and drink into the hamper, and proceeded to go with it forth. And

nothing was ever more wonderful to Lludd, than that
the hamper should hold so much.

And thereupon King Lludd went after him and
spoke unto him thus. "Stop, stop," said he,
"though thou hast done many insults and much
spoil erewhile, thou shalt not do so any more, unless

thy skill in arms and thy prowess be greater than
mine."

Then he instantly put down the hamper on the
floor, and awaited him. And a fierce encounter was
between them, so that the glittering fire flew out from
their arms. And at the last Lludd grappled with
him, and fate bestowed the victory on Lludd. And
he threw the plague to the earth. And after he had

overcome him by strength and might, he besought his mercy. "How can I grant thee mercy," said the king, "after all the many injuries and wrongs that thou hast done me?" "All the losses that ever I have caused thee," said he, "I will make thee atonement for, equal to what I have taken. And I will never do the like from this time forth. But thy faithful vassal will I be." And the king accepted this from him.

And thus Lludd freed the Island of Britain from the three plagues. And from thenceforth until the end of his life, in prosperous peace did Lludd the son of Beli rule the Island of Britain. And this Tale is called the Story of Lludd and Llevelys. And thus it ends.

TALIESIN.

In times past there lived in Penllyn a man of gentle lineage, named Tegid Voel, and his dwelling was in the midst of the Lake Tegid, and his wife was called Caridwen. And there was born to him of his wife a

son named Morvran ab Tegid, and also a daughter
named Creirwy, the fairest maiden in the world was
she; and they had a brother the most ill-favoured
man in the world, Avagddu. Now Caridwen his
mother thought that he was not likely to be admitted
among men of noble birth, by reason of his ugliness,
unless he had some exalted merits or knowledge.
For it was in the beginning of Arthur's time and of
the Round Table.

So she resolved, according to the arts of the books
of the Fferyllt,[1] to boil a cauldron of Inspiration and
Science for her son, that his reception might be
honourable because of his knowledge of the mysteries
of the future state of the world.

Then she began to boil the cauldron, which from
the beginning of its boiling might not cease to boil
for a year and a day, until three blessed drops were
obtained of the grace of inspiration.

And she put Gwion Bach the son of Gwreang of
Llanfair in Caereinion, in Powys, to stir the cauldron,
and a blind man named Morda to kindle the fire
beneath it, and she charged them that they should
not suffer it to cease boiling for the space of a year
and a day. And she herself, according to the books
of the astronomers, and in planetary hours, gathered
every day of all charm-bearing herbs. And one day,
towards the end of the year, as Caridwen was culling
plants and making incantations, it chanced that three
drops of the charmed liquor flew out of the cauldron
and fell upon the finger of Gwion Bach. And by
reason of their great heat he put his finger to his
'mouth,[2] and the instant he put those marvel-working

---

[1] Of the books of the magician. [Vergil = Fferyllt = magician
or chemist.]   [2] Head.

drops into his mouth, he foresaw everything that was
to come, and perceived that his chief care must be to
guard against the wiles of Caridwen, for vast was her
skill.   And in very great fear he fled towards his own
land.   And the cauldron burst in two, because all
the liquor within it except the three charm-bearing
drops was poisonous, so that the horses of Gwyddno

Garanhir were poisoned by the water of the stream
into which the liquor of the cauldron ran, and the
confluence of that stream was called the Poison of the
Horses of Gwyddno from that time forth.
    Thereupon came in Caridwen and saw all the toil
of the whole year lost.   And she seized a billet of

wood and struck the blind Morda on the head until one of his eyes fell out upon his cheek. And he said, "Wrongfully hast thou disfigured me, for I am innocent. Thy loss was not because of me." "Thou speakest truth," said Caridwen, "it was Gwion Bach who robbed me."

And she went forth after him, running. And he saw her, and changed himself into a hare and fled. But she changed herself into a greyhound and turned him. And he ran towards a river, and became a fish. And she in the form of an otter-bitch chased him under the water, until he was fain to turn himself into a bird of the air. Then she, as a hawk, followed him and gave him no rest in the sky. And just as she was about to stoop upon him, and he was in fear of death, he espied a heap of winnowed wheat on the floor of a barn, and he dropped amongst the wheat, and turned himself into one of the grains. Then she transformed herself into a high-crested black hen, and went to the wheat and scratched it with her feet, and found him out and swallowed him. And, as the story says, she bore him nine months, and when she was delivered of him, she could not find it in her heart to kill him, by reason of his beauty. So she wrapped him in a leathern bag, and cast him into the sea to the mercy of God, on the twenty-ninth day of April.

And at that time the weir of Gwyddno was on the strand between Dyvi and Aberystwyth, near to his own castle, and the value of an hundred pounds was taken in that weir every May eve. And in those days Gwyddno had an only son named Elphin, the most hapless of youths, and the most needy. And it grieved his father sore, for he thought that he was

born in an evil hour. And by the advice of his
council, his father had granted him the drawing of
the weir that year, to see if good luck would ever
befall him, and to give him something wherewith to
begin the world.

And the next day, when Elphin went to look, there
was nothing in the weir. But as he turned back he
perceived the leathern bag upon a pole of the weir.
Then said one of the weir-ward unto Elphin, "Thou
wast never unlucky until to-night, and now thou hast
destroyed the virtues of the weir, which always yielded
the value of an hundred pounds every May eve, and

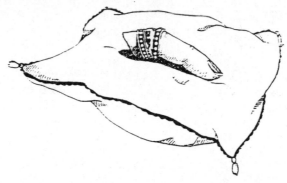

to-night there is nothing but this leathern skin within
it." "How now," said Elphin, "there may be therein the value of an hundred pounds." Well! they
took up the leathern bag, and he who opened it saw
the forehead of the boy, and said to Elphin, "Behold
a radiant brow!"[1] "Taliesin be he called," said
Elphin. And he lifted the boy in his arms, and
lamenting his mischance, he placed him sorrowfully

[1] Taliesin

behind him. And he made his horse amble gently, that before had been trotting, and he carried him as softly as if he had been sitting in the easiest chair in the world. And presently the boy made a Consolation and praise to Elphin, and foretold honour to Elphin; and the Consolation was as you may see,

"Fair Elphin cease to lament!
Let no one be dissatisfied with his own,
To despair will bring no advantage.
No man sees what supports him;
The prayer of Cynllo will not be in vain;
God will not violate his promise.
Never in Gwyddno's weir
Was there such good luck as this night.
Fair Elphin, dry thy cheeks!
Being too sad will not avail,
Although thou thinkest thou hast no gain,
Too much grief will bring thee no good;
Nor doubt the miracles of the Almighty:
Although I am but little, I am highly gifted.
From seas, and from mountains,
And from the depths of rivers,
God brings wealth to the fortunate man.
Elphin of lively qualities,
Thy resolution is unmanly;
Thou must not be over sorrowful:
Better to trust in God than to forbode ill.
Weak and small as I am,
On the foaming beach of the ocean,
In the day of trouble, I shall be
Of more service to thee than 300 salmon.
Elphin of notable qualities,
Be not displeased at thy misfortune;
Although reclined thus weak in my bag,
There lies a virtue in my tongue.
While I continue thy protector
Thou hast not much to fear;
Remembering the names of the Trinity,
None shall be able to harm thee."

And this was the first poem that Taliesin ever sang, being to console Elphin in his grief for that the produce of the weir was lost, and, what was worse, that all the world would consider that it was through his fault and ill-luck. And then Gwyddno Garanhir[1] asked him what he was, whether man or spirit. Whereupon he sang this tale, and said,

" First, I have been formed a comely person,
  In the court of Ceridwen I have done penance ;
  Though little I was seen, placidly received,
  I was great on the floor of the place to where I was led ;
  I have been a prized defence, the sweet muse the cause,
  And by law without speech I have been liberated
  By a smiling black old hag, when irritated
  Dreadful her claim when pursued :
  I have fled with vigour, I have fled as a frog,
  I have fled in the semblance of a crow, scarcely finding rest ;
  I have fled vehemently, I have fled as a chain,
  I have fled as a roe into an entangled thicket ;
  I have fled as a wolf cub, I have fled as a wolf in a wilderness,
  I have fled as a thrush of portending language ;
  I have fled as a fox, used to concurrent bounds of quirks ;
  I have fled as a martin, which did not avail :
  I have fled as a squirrel, that vainly hides,
  I have fled as a stag's antler, of ruddy course,
  I have fled as iron in a glowing fire, .
  I have fled as a spear-head, of woe to such as has a wish for it ;
  I have fled as a fierce bull bitterly fighting,
  I have fled as a bristly boar seen in a ravine,
  I have fled as a white grain of pure wheat,
  On the skirt of a hempen sheet entangled,
  That seemed of the size of a mare's foal,
  That is filling like a ship on the waters ;
  Into a dark leathern bag I was thrown,
  And on a boundless sea I was sent adrift ;
  Which was to me an omen of being tenderly nursed,
  And the Lord God then set me at liberty."

---

[1] This should be Elphin son of Gwyddno.

Then came Elphin to the house or court of
Gwyddno his father, and Taliesin with him. And
Gwyddno asked him if he had had a good haul at the
weir, and he told him that he had got that which was
better than fish. "What was that?" said Gwyddno.
"A Bard," answered Elphin. Then said Gwyddno,
"Alas, what will he profit thee?" And Taliesin
himself replied and said, "He will profit him more
than the weir ever profited thee." Asked Gwyddno,
"Art thou able to speak, and thou so little?" And
Taliesin answered him, "I am better able to speak
than thou to question me." "Let me hear what thou
canst say," quoth Gwyddno. Then Taliesin sang,—

" In water there is a quality endowed with a blessing ;
   On God it is most just to meditate aright ;
   To God it is proper to supplicate with seriousness,
   Since no obstacle can there be to obtain a reward from him.
   Three times have I been born, I know by meditation ;
   It were miserable for a person not to come and obtain
   All the sciences of the world, collected together in my breast,
   For I know what has been, what in future will occur.
   I will supplicate my Lord that I get refuge in him,
   A regard I may obtain in his grace ;
   The Son of Mary is my trust, great in Him is my delight,
   For in Him is the world continually upholden.
   God has been to instruct me and to raise my expectation,
   The true Creator of heaven, who affords me protection ;
   It is rightly intended that the saints should daily pray,
   For God, the renovator, will bring them to him."

*   *   *   *   *   *

And forthwith Elphin gave his haul to his wife, and
she nursed him tenderly and lovingly. Thence-
forward Elphin increased in riches more and more
day after day, and in love and favour with the king,
and there abode Taliesin until he was thirteen years
old, when Elphin son of Gwyddno went by a

Christmas invitation to his uncle, Maelgwn Gwynedd,
who sometime after this held open court at Christmas-
tide in the castle of Dyganwy, for all the number
of his lords of both degrees, both spiritual and
temporal, with a vast and thronged host of knights
and squires.   And amongst them there arose a discourse
and discussion.   And thus was it said.

"Is there in the whole world a king so great as
Maelgwn, or one on whom Heaven has bestowed so
many spiritual gifts as upon him?   First, form, and
beauty, and meekness, and strength, besides all the
powers of the soul?"   And together with these they
said that Heaven had given one gift that exceeded all
the others, which was the beauty, and comeliness,
and grace, and wisdom, and modesty of his queen;
whose virtues surpassed those of all the ladies and
noble maidens throughout the whole kingdom.   And
with this they put questions one to another amongst
themselves, Who had braver men?   Who had fairer
or swifter horses or greyhounds?   Who had more
skilful or wiser bards—than Maelgwn?

Now at that time the bards were in great favour
with the exalted of the kingdom; and then none
performed the office of those who are now called
heralds, unless they were learned men, not only
expert in the service of kings and princes, but
studious and well versed in the lineage, and arms, and
exploits of princes and kings, and in discussions
concerning foreign kingdoms, and the ancient things
of this kingdom, and chiefly in the annals of the first
nobles; and also were prepared always with their
answers in various languages, Latin, French, Welsh,
and English.   And together with this they were great
chroniclers, and recorders, and skilful in framing

verses, and ready in making englyns in every one of
these languages. Now of these there were at that
feast within the palace of Maelgwn as many as four
and twenty, and chief of them all, was one named
Heinin Vardd.

When they had all made an end of thus praising
the king and his gifts, it befell that Elphin spoke on
this wise. "Of a truth none but a king may vie with
a king; but were he not a king, I would say that my
wife was as virtuous as any lady in the kingdom, and
also that I have a bard who is more skilful than all
the king's bards." In a short space some of his
fellows showed the king all the boastings of Elphin;
and the king ordered him to be thrown into a strong
prison, until he might know the truth as to the virtues
of his wife, and the wisdom of his bard.

Now when Elphin had been put in a tower of the
castle, with a thick chain about his feet, (it is said that
it was a silver chain, because he was of royal blood;)
the king, as the story relates, sent his son Rhun to
enquire into the demeanour of Elphin's wife. Now
Rhun was the most graceless man in the world, and
there was neither wife nor maiden with whom he had
held converse, but was evil spoken of. While Rhun
went in haste towards Elphin's dwelling, being fully
minded to bring disgrace upon his wife, Taliesin told
his mistress how that the king had placed his master
in durance in prison, and how that Rhun was coming
in haste to strive to bring disgrace upon her. Wherefore he caused his mistress to array one of the maids
of her kitchen in her apparel; which the noble lady
gladly did; and she loaded her hands with the best
rings that she and her husband possessed.

In this guise Taliesin caused his mistress to put the

maiden to sit at the board in her room at supper, and
he made her to seem as her mistress, and the mistress
to seem as the maid. And when they were in due
time seated at their supper in the manner that has
been said, Rhun suddenly arrived at Elphin's dwelling, and was received with joy, for all the servants
knew him plainly; and they brought him in haste to
the room of their mistress, in the semblance of whom
the maid rose up from supper and welcomed him
gladly. And afterwards she sat down to supper again
the second time, and Rhun with her. Then Rhun
began jesting with the maid, who still kept the
semblance of her mistress. And verily this story
shows that the maiden became so intoxicated, that
she fell asleep; and the story relates that it was a
powder that Rhun put into the drink, that made her
sleep so soundly that she never felt it when he cut
from off her hand her little finger, whereon was the
signet ring of Elphin, which he had sent to his wife
as a token, a short time before. And Rhun returned
to the king with the finger and the ring as a proof, to
show that he had cut it from off her hand, without
her awaking from her sleep of intemperance.

The king rejoiced greatly at these tidings, and he
sent for his councillors, to whom he told the whole
story from the beginning. And he caused Elphin to
be brought out of his prison, and he chided him
because of his boast. And he spake unto Elphin on
this wise. "Elphin, be it known to thee beyond a
doubt that it is but folly for a man to trust in the
virtues of his wife further than he can see her; and
that thou mayest be certain of thy wife's vileness,
behold her finger, with thy signet ring upon it, which
was cut from her hand last night, while she slept the

sleep of intoxication." Then thus spake Elphin.
"With thy leave, mighty king, I cannot deny my
ring, for it is known of many; but verily I assert
strongly that the finger around which it is, was never
attached to the hand of my wife, for in truth and
certainty there are three notable things pertaining to
it, none of which ever belonged to any of my wife's
fingers. The first of the three is, that it is certain,
by your grace's leave, that wheresocver my wife is at
this present hour, whether sitting, or standing, or
lying down, this ring would never remain upon her
thumb, whereas you can plainly see that it was hard
to draw it over the joint of the little finger of the
hand whence this was cut; the second thing is, that
my wife has never let pass one Saturday since I have
known her without paring her nails before going to
bed, and you can see fully that the nail of this little
finger has not been pared for a month. The third
is, truly, that the hand whence this finger came was
kneading rye dough within three days before the
finger was cut therefrom, and I can assure your
goodness that my wife has never kneaded rye dough
since my wife she has been."

Then the king was mightily wrath with Elphin for
so stoutly withstanding him, respecting the goodness of his wife, wherefore he ordered him to his
prison a second time, saying that he should not be
loosed thence until he had proved the truth of his
boast, as well concerning the wisdom of his bard as
the virtues of his wife.

In the meantime his wife and Taliesin remained
joyful at Elphin's dwelling. And Taliesin shewed his
mistress how that Elphin was in prison because of
them, but he bade her be glad for that he would go

to Maelgwn's court to free his master. Then she
asked him in what manner he would set him free.
And he answered her,—

> " A journey will I perform,
> And to the gate I will come ;
> The hall I will enter,
> And my song I will sing ;
> My speech I will pronounce
> To silence royal bards.
> In presence of their chief,
> I will greet to deride,
> Upon them I will break
> And Elphin I will free.
> Should contention arise,
> In presence of the prince,
> With summons to the bards
> For the sweet flowing song,
> And wizards' posing lore
> And wisdom of Druids.
> In the court of the sons of the distributor
> Some are who did appear
> Intent on wily schemes,
> By craft and tricking means,
> In pangs of affliction
> To wrong the innocent,
> Let the fools be silent, —
> As erst in Badon's fight, —
> With Arthur of liberal ones
> The head, with long red blades ;
> Through feats of testy men,
> And a chief with his foes.
> Woe be to them, the fools,
> When revenge comes on them.
> I Taliesin, chief of bards,
> With a sapient druid's words,
> Will set kind Elphin free
> From haughty tyrant's bonds.
> To their fell and chilling cry,
> By the act of a surprising steed,
> From the far distant North,
> There soon shall be an end.

I

Let neither grace nor health
Be to Maelgwn Gwynedd,
For this force and this wrong ;
And be extremes of ills
And an avenged end
To Rhun and all his race :
Short be his course of life,
Be all his lands laid waste ;
And long exile be assigned
To Maelgwn Gwynedd !"

After this he took leave of his mistress, and came at last to the court of Maelgwn, who was going to sit in his hall and dine in his royal state, as it was the custom in those days for kings and princes to do at every chief feast. And as soon as Taliesin entered the hall, he placed himself in a quiet corner, near the place where the bards and the minstrels were wont to come to in doing their service and duty to the king, as is the custom at the high festivals when the bounty is proclaimed. And so, when the bards and the heralds came to cry largess and to proclaim the power of the king and his strength, at the moment that they passed by the corner wherein he was crouching, Taliesin pouted out his lips after them, and played "Blerwm, blerwm," with his finger upon his lips. Neither took they much notice of him as they went by, but proceeded forward till they came before the king, unto whom they made their obeisance with their bodies, as they were wont, without speaking a single word, but pouting out their lips, and making mouths at the king, playing "Blerwm, blerwm," upon their lips with their fingers, as they had seen the boy do elsewhere. This sight caused the king to wonder and to deem within himself that they were drunk with many liquors. Wherefore he commanded one of his lords, who served at the board, to go to them and desire them to collect their wits, and to consider where they stood, and what it was fitting for them to do. And this lord did so gladly. But they ceased not from their folly any more than before. Whereupon he sent to them a second time, and a third, desiring them to go forth from the hall. At the last the king ordered one of his squires to give a blow to the chief of them named Heinin Vardd; and the squire took a broom, and struck him on the head, so that he fell back in his seat. Then he arose and went on his knees, and besought leave of the king's grace to show that this their fault was not through want of knowledge, neither through drunkenness, but by the influence of some spirit that was in the hall. And after this Heinin spoke on this wise. "Oh honourable king, be it known to your grace, that not from the strength of drink, or of too much liquor, are we dumb, without power of speech like drunken men, but through the influence of a spirit that sits in the corner yonder in the form of a child." Forthwith the king commanded the squire to fetch him; and he went to the nook where Taliesin sat, and brought him before the king, who asked him what he was, and whence he came. And he answered the king in verse.

" Primary chief bard am I to Elphin,
And my original country is the region of the summer stars ;
Idno and Heinin called me Merddin,
At length every king will call me Taliesin.

I was with my Lord in the highest sphere,
On the fall of Lucifer into the depth of hell :
I have borne a banner before Alexander ;
I know the names of the stars from north to south ;

I have been on the galaxy at the throne of the Distributor ;
I was in Canaan when Absalom was slain ;
I conveyed the divine Spirit to the level of the vale of Hebron ;
I was in the court of Don before the birth of Gwydion.
I was instructor to Eli and Enoc ;
I have been winged by the genius of the splendid crosier ;
I have been loquacious prior to being gifted with speech ;
I was at the place of the crucifixion of the merciful Son of God ;
I have been three periods in the prison of Arianrod ;
I have been the chief director of the work of the tower of
    Nimrod ;
I am a wonder whose origin is not known.

I have been in Asia with Noah in the ark,
I have seen the destruction of Sodom and Gomorra ;
I have been in India when Roma was built,
I am now come here to the remnant of Troia.

I have been with my Lord in the manger of the ass ;
I strengthened Moses through the water of Jordan ;
I have been in the firmament with Mary Magdalene ;
I have obtained the muse from the cauldron of Ceridwen ;
I have been bard of the harp to Lleon of Lochlin.
I have been on the White Hill, in the court of Cynvelyn,
For a day and a year in stocks and fetters,
I have suffered hunger for the Son of the Virgin.
I have been fostered in the land of the Deity,
I have been teacher to all intelligences,
I am able to instruct the whole universe.
I shall be until the day of doom on the face of the earth ;
And it is not known whether my body is flesh or fish.

> Then I was for nine months
> In the womb of the hag Ceridwen ;
> I was originally little Gwion,
> And at length I am Taliesin."

And when the king and his nobles had heard the
song, they wondered much, for they had never heard
the like from a boy so young as he. And when the
king knew that he was the bard of Elphin, he bade

Heinin, his first and wisest bard, to answer Taliesin
and to strive with him.   But when he came, he could
do no other, but play "blerwm" on his lips; and
when he sent for the others of the four and twenty
bards, they all did likewise, and could do no other.
And Maelgwn asked the boy Taliesin what was his
errand, and he answered him in song.

> " Puny bards, I am trying
>   To secure the prize, if I can ;
>   By a gentle prophetic strain
>   I am endeavouring to retrieve
>   The loss I may have suffered ;
>   Complete the attempt, I hope,
>   Since Elphin endures trouble
>   In the fortress of Teganwy,
>   On him may there not be laid
>   Too many chains and fetters ;
>   The Chair of the fortress of Teganwy
>   Will I again seek ;
>   Strengthened by my muse I am powerful ;
>   Mighty on my part is what I seek,
>   For three hundred songs and more
>   Are combined in the spell I sing.
>   There ought not to stand where I am
>   Neither stone, neither ring ;
>   And there ought not to be about me
>   Any bard who may not know
>   That Elphin the son of Gwyddno
>   Is in the land of Artro,
>   Secured by thirteen locks,
>   For praising his instructor ;
>   And then I Taliesin,
>   Chief of the bards of the west,
>   Shall loosen Elphin
>   Out of a golden fetter."

*   *   *   *

> " If you be primary bards
>   To the master of sciences,
>   Declare ye mysteries

That relate to the inhabitants of the world ;
There is a noxious creature,
From the rampart of Satanas,
Which has overcome all
Between the deep and the shallow ;
Equally wide are his jaws
As the mountains of the Alps ;
Him death will not subdue,
Nor hand or blades ;
There is the load of nine hundred waggons
In the hair of his two paws ;
There is in his head an eye
Green as the limpid sheet of icicle ;
Three springs arise
In the nape of his neck ;
Sea-roughs thereon
Swim through it ;
There was the dissolution of the oxen
Of Deividonwy the water-gifted.
The names of the three springs
From the midst of the ocean ;
One generated brine
Which is from the Corina,
To replenish the flood
Over seas disappearing ;
The second, without injury
It will fall on us,
When there is rain abroad.
Through the whelming sky ;
The third will appear
Through the mountain veins,
Like a flinty banquet.
The work of the King of kings.
You are blundering bards,
In too much solicitude ;
You cannot celebrate
The kingdom of the Britons ;
And I am Taliesin,
Chief of the bards of the west,
Who will loosen Elphin
Out of the golden fetter."

     *   *   *

"Be silent, then, ye unlucky rhyming bards,
For you cannot judge between truth and falsehood.
If you be primary bards formed by Heaven,
Tell your king what his fate will be.
It is I who am a diviner and a leading bard,
And know every passage in the country of your king;
I shall liberate Elphin from the belly of the stony tower;
And will tell your king what will befall him.
A most strange creature will come from the sea marsh of
  Rhianedd
As a punishment of iniquity on Maelgwn Gwynedd;
His hair, his teeth, and his eyes being as gold,
And this will bring destruction upon Maelgwn Gwynedd."

       *   *   *   *

"Discover thou what is
The strong creature from before the flood,
Without flesh, without bone,
Without vein, without blood,
Without head, without feet;
It will neither be older nor younger
Than at the beginning;
For fear of a denial,
There are no rude wants
With creatures.
Great God! how the sea whitens
When first it come!
Great are its gusts
When it comes from the south;
Great are its evaporations
When it strikes on coasts.
It is in the field, it is in the wood,
Without hand and without foot,
Without signs of old age,
Though it be co-eval
With the five ages or periods;
And older still,
Though they be numberless years.
It is also so wide
As the surface of the earth;
And it was not born,
Nor was it seen.
It will cause consternation

Wherever God willeth.
On sea, and on land,
It neither sees, nor is seen.
Its course is devious,
And will not come when desired.
On land and on sea,
It is indispensible.
It is without an equal,
It is four-sided ;
It is not confined,
It is incomparable ;
It comes from four quarters
It will not be advised,
It will not be without advice.
It commences its journey
Above the marble rock.[1]
It is sonorous, it is dumb,
It is mild,
It is strong, it is bold,
When it glances over the land.
It is silent, it is vocal,
It is clamorous,
It is the most noisy
On the face of the earth.
It is good, it is bad,
It is extremely injurious.
It is concealed,
Because sight cannot perceive it.
It is noxious, it is beneficial ;
It is yonder, it is here ;
It will discompose,
But will not repair the injury ;
It will not suffer for its doings,
Seeing it is blameless.
It is wet, it is dry,
It frequently comes,
Proceeding from the heat of the sun,
And the coldness of the moon.
The moon is less beneficial,
Inasmuch as her heat is less.

---

[1] Possibly an allusion to the Cave of Æolus.

One Being has prepared it,
Out of all creatures,
By a tremendous blast,
To wreak vengeance
On Maelgwn Gwynedd."

And while he was thus singing his verse near the door there arose a mighty storm of wind, so that the king and all his nobles thought that the castle would fall upon their heads. And the king caused them to fetch Elphin in haste from his dungeon, and placed him before Taliesin. And it is said that immediately he sang a verse, so that the chains opened from about his feet.

" I adore the Supreme, Lord of all animation,—
Him that supports the heaven, Ruler of every extreme,
Him that made the water good for all,
Him who has bestowed each gift, and blesses it ;—
May abundance of mead be given Maelgwn of Anglesey, who
  supplies us,
From his foaming meadhorns, with the choicest pure liquor.
Since bees collect, and do not enjoy,
We have sparkling distilled mead, which is universally praised.
The multitude of creatures which the earth nourishes,
God made for man, with a view to enrich him ;—
Some are violent, some are mute, he enjoys them,
Some are wild, some are tame ; the Lord makes them ;—
Part of their produce becomes clothing ;
For food and beverage till doom will they continue.
I entreat the Supreme, Sovereign of the region of peace,
To liberate Elphin from banishment,
The man who gave me wine, and ale, and mead,
With large princely steeds, of beautiful appearance ;
May he yet give me ; and at the end,
May God of His good will grant me, in honour,
A succession of numberless ages, in the retreat of tranquil-
  lity.—
Elphin, knight of mead, late be thy dissolution !"

And afterwards he sang the ode which is called
"The Excellence of the Bards."

> " What was the first man
> Made by the God of heaven ;
> What the fairest flattering speech
> That was prepared by Ieuav ;
> What meat, what drink,
> What roof his shelter ;
> What the first impression
> Of his primary thinking ;
> What became his clothing ;
> Who carried on a disguise,
> Owing to the wiles of the country,
> In the beginning ?
> Wherefore should a stone be hard ;
> Why should a thorn be sharp-pointed ;
> Who is hard like a flint ;
> Who is salt like brine ;
> Who sweet like honey ;
> Who rides on the gale ;
>
> Why ridged should be the nose ;
> Why should a wheel be round ;
> Why should the tongue be gifted with speech
> Rather than another member ?
> If thy bards, Heinin, be competent,
> Let them reply to me, Taliesin."

And after that he sang the address which is called
"The Reproof of the Bards."

> " If thou art a bard completely imbued
> With genius not to be controlled,
> Be thou not untractable
> Within the court of thy king ;
> Until thy rigmarole shall be known,
> Be thou silent Heinin
> As to the name of thy verse,
> And the name of thy vaunting ;

And as to the name of thy grandsire
Prior to his being baptized.
And the name of the sphere,
And the name of the element,
And the name of thy language,
And the name of thy region.
Avaunt, ye bards above,
Avaunt, ye bards below !
My beloved is below,
In the fetter of Arianrod.
It is certain you know not
How to understand the song I utter,
Nor clearly how to discriminate
Between the truth and what is false ;
Puny bards, crows of the district,
Why do you not take to flight ?
A bard that will not silence me,
Silence may he not obtain,
Till he goes to be covered
Under gravel and pebbles ;
Such as shall listen to me,
May God listen to him."

Then sang he the piece called "The Spite of the Bards."

"Minstrels persevere in their false custom,
Immoral ditties are their delight ;
Vain and tasteless praise they recite ;
Falsehood at all times do they utter ;
The innocent persons they ridicule ;
Married women they destroy,
Innocent virgins of Mary they corrupt ;
As they pass their lives away in vanity ;
Poor innocent persons they ridicule ;
At night they get drunk, they sleep the day ;
In idleness without work they feed themselves ;
The Church they hate, and the tavern they frequent ;
With thieves and perjured fellows they associate ;
At courts they inquire after feasts ;
Every senseless word they bring forward ;
Every deadly sin they praise ;

Every vile course of life they lead ;
Through every village, town, and country they stroll ;
Concerning the gripe of death they think not ;
Neither lodging nor charity do they give ;
Indulging in victuals to excess.
Psalms or prayers they do not use,
Tithes or offerings to God they do not pay,
On holidays or Sundays they do not worship ;
Vigils or festivals they do not heed.
The birds do fly, the fish do swim,
The bees collect honey, worms do crawl,
Every thing travails to obtain its food,
Except minstrels and lazy useless thieves.

I deride neither song nor minstrelsy,
For they are given by God to lighten thought ;
But him who abuses them,
For blaspheming Jesus and his service."

Taliesin having set his master free from prison, and having protected the innocence of his wife, and silenced the Bards so that not one of them dared to say a word, now brought Elphin's wife before them, and shewed that she had not one finger wanting. Right glad was Elphin, right glad was Taliesin.

Then he bade Elphin wager the king, that he had a horse both better and swifter than the king's horses. And this Elphin did, and the day, and the time, and the place were fixed, and the place was that which at this day is called Morva Rhiannedd ; and thither the king went with all his people, and four and twenty of the swiftest horses he possessed. And after a long process the course was marked, and the horses were placed for running. Then came Taliesin with four and twenty twigs of holly, which he had burnt black, and he caused the youth who was to ride his master's horse to place them in his belt, and he gave him orders to let all the king's horses get before him, and as he should overtake one horse after the other, to take one of the twigs and strike the horse with it over the crupper, and then let that twig fall; and after that to take another twig, and do in like manner to every one of the horses, as he should overtake them, enjoining the horseman strictly to watch when his own horse should stumble, and to throw down his cap on the spot. All these things did the youth fulfil, giving a blow to every one of the king's horses, and throwing down his cap on the spot where his horse stumbled. And to this spot Taliesin brought his master after his horse had won the race. And he caused Elphin to put workmen to dig a hole there; and when they had dug the ground deep enough, they found a large cauldron full of gold. And then said Taliesin, " Elphin, behold a payment and reward unto thee, for having taken me out of the weir, and for having reared me from that time until now." And on this spot stands a pool of water, which is to this time called Pwllbair.

After all this, the king caused Taliesin to be brought before him, and he asked him to recite concerning the creation of man from the beginning; and thereupon he made the poem which is now called "One of the Four Pillars of Song."

" The Almighty made,
Down the Hebron vale,
With his plastic hands,
Adam's fair form ;

And five hundred years,
Void of any help,
There he remained and lay
Without a soul.

He again did form,
In calm paradise,
From a left-side rib,
Bliss-throbbing Eve.

Seven hours they were
The orchard keeping,
Till Satan brought strife,
With wiles from hell.

Thence were they driven,
Cold and shivering,
To gain their living,
　Into this world.

To bring forth with pain
Their sons and daughters,
To have possession
　Of Asia's land.

Twice five, ten and eight,
She was self-bearing,
The mixed burden
　Of man-woman.

And once, not hidden,
She brought forth Abel,
And Cain the forlorn,
　The homicide.

To him and his mate
Was given a spade,
To break up the soil,
　Thus to get bread.

The wheat pure and white,
Summer tilth to sow,
Every man to feed,
　Till great yule feast.

An angelic hand
From the high Father,
Brought seed for growing
　That Eve might sow;

But she then did hide
Of the gift a tenth,
And all did not sow
　Of what was dug.

Black rye then was found,
And not pure wheat grain,
To show the mischief
　Thus of thieving.

For this thievish act,
It is requisite,
That all men should pay
　Tithe unto God.

Of the ruddy wine,
Planted on sunny days,
And on new moon nights;
　And the white wine.

The wheat rich in grain
And red flowing wine
Christ's pure body make,
　Son of Alpha.

The wafer is flesh,
The wine is spilt blood,
The Trinity's words
　Sanctify them.

The concealed books
From Emmanuel's hand
Were brought by Raphael
　As Adam's gift.

When in his old age,
To his chin immersed
In Jordan's water,
　Keeping a fast,

Moses did obtain,
In Jordan's water,
The aid of the three
　Most special rods.

Solomon did obtain,
In Babel's tower,
All the sciences
　In Asia land.

So did I obtain,
In my bardic books,
All the sciences
　Of Europe and Africa.

Their course, their bearing
Their permitted way,
And their fate I know,
   Unto the end.

Oh ! what misery,
Through extreme of woe,
Prophecy will show
   On Troia's race !

A coiling serpent,
Proud and merciless,
On her golden wings,
   From Germany.

She will overrun
England and Scotland,
From Lychlyn sea-shore
   To the Severn.

Then will the Brython
Be as prisoners,
By strangers swayed,
   From Saxony.

Their Lord they will praise,
Their speech they will keep
Their land they will lose,
   Except wild Walia.

Till some change shall come,
After long penance,
When equally rife
   The two crimes come.

Britons then shall have
Their land and their crown,
And the strangers swarm
   Shall disappear.

All the angel's words,
As to peace and war,
Will be fulfilled
   To Britain's race.

He further told the king various prophecies of
things that should be in the world, in songs, as
follows.

* * * * * *